THE SILK THREAD

Rowan Bennet

Text and images copyright © 2026 by Rowan Bennet

First paperback edition January 2026

ISBN 9780956710840

Published by Second Needle

www.secondneedle.com

CHAPTER 1

The Ashworth bequest arrived on a Tuesday in late October, forty-three boxes of moderate interest and indifferent provenance. Anna signed for them in the loading bay, checked the seals against the transfer manifest, and spent the rest of the morning moving them into the processing queue behind a sixteenth-century herbal that actually mattered and a water-damaged collection of estate papers that nobody wanted but the university had accepted anyway out of politeness to a dying alumnus.

She didn't get to the Ashworth materials until the following week. By then the October rain had settled into the permanent grey drizzle of early November, and the conservation workroom had taken on the chill that meant the heating system was arguing with itself again. Anna wore fingerless gloves at her bench—not ideal for delicate work, but better than numb hands.

The Ashworth family had been minor Oxfordshire gentry, the sort who accumulated possessions through inheritance rather than intention. Three generations of moderate education and no particular curiosity had produced a collection that was, by archival standards, perfectly adequate: family correspondence, household accounts, the usual Victorian obsession with documenting every expenditure from coal deliveries to calling cards. There would be nothing revelatory here. There rarely was.

Anna worked methodically through the first box, then the second. Condition reports, provenance notes, the patient archaeology of paper and binding she'd built a career on. She could read a book's history in its construction—where pages were thumbed soft, where binding showed stress, what marginalia revealed about the hands that had held it before. Most conservators developed this instinct eventually. Anna had always had it, the way some people had perfect pitch.

The botanical textbook was in the seventh box, nestled between a household recipe collection and someone's incomplete attempt at a family genealogy. *Flora of the British Isles*, 1876, quarter-bound in green cloth with marbled boards. Anna noted moderate foxing on the preliminary pages, some amateur pressings between leaves—wildflowers, she thought, probably collected by a child or a bored wife on country walks. The spine was intact but loosening. Routine.

She opened the back cover to check for bookplates or ownership inscriptions and found the pocket.

This wasn't unusual. Victorians often modified their books, adding pockets or folders for keeping related correspondence, receipts, notes. Anna had seen hundreds of them. She slipped two fingers into the opening, expecting a few letters about seed catalogues or garden planning.

The paper that came out was high quality. Heavy stock, deckle-edged, the kind used for personal correspondence rather than business. A small bundle of letters, perhaps a dozen, tied with faded ribbon that had once been blue.

Anna untied the ribbon carefully—it was fragile, apt to split —and unfolded the first letter. The hand was feminine, educated, the ink brown with age but still legible. She began reading automatically, her eyes catching dates and salutations before her mind fully engaged.

November 3rd, 1887

My dearest—

Anna's gaze moved down the page, still in cataloguing mode, noting the paper's condition, the consistency of the hand.

I have thought of nothing but Thursday since you left me. You must know this. You must feel it too, this thread that stretches between us even now, even as I write these words knowing you will not read them for days. I am yours across any distance. I am yours in the spaces between heartbeats.

Anna stopped reading.

She looked up — an automatic reflex, as though someone might be watching — and Marcus was still at the far bench with his earphones in, oblivious. Through the high windows, grey light fell on grey stone.

She looked back at the letter.

You told me to be patient. I am trying. But patience is a discipline I have not yet mastered, not in this. Not when I can still feel where your hands rested at my waist. Not when I close my eyes and see—

Anna folded the letter.

Her face was warm. She was, she realised, holding her breath.

These were personal letters. Intimate ones. They surfaced sometimes in family collections — usually husbands to wives, occasionally between men in language careful enough to fool everyone who wasn't looking for it. The protocol was straightforward: note them in the catalogue, flag them for the special collections librarian, restrict access if the content warranted. The protocol did not include reading the rest of the bundle alone at her bench.

Anna set the bundle aside and returned to the botanical textbook. She completed her condition report: binding loosening, foxing present, amateur pressings between pages 47-48, 112-113, and 156-157. Paper pocket added to rear endpaper, containing correspondence —she paused, pen hovering—*personal correspondence, approximately twelve items, nineteenth century, requires further assessment.*

Further assessment. That was professional language for *I need to read these properly*.

She finished the report. Set the textbook in the processed pile. Moved on to the genealogy, which was dull and incomplete and exactly what she needed to clear her head.

But she kept glancing at the bundle of letters, sitting at the corner of her bench where she'd placed them. The faded ribbon. The heavy paper.

I am yours across any distance.

Anna had handled hundreds of Victorian letters. Thousands. She knew their conventions, their circumlocutions, the elaborate dance of propriety and feeling that characterised the period's correspondence. She had read love letters before—passionate ones, restrained ones, letters that burned with feeling and letters that smothered it under layers of acceptable sentiment.

This felt different.

She couldn't have said why, not yet. Something in the cadence. Something in the particular weight of *I am yours*.

At half past four, Marcus left for the day. Anna stayed, ostensibly to finish processing box seven. She waited until she heard his footsteps fade down the corridor, until the door clicked shut behind him.

Then she reached for the letters.

The reading room was the right place for this. Support cushions, appropriate lighting, the whole protocol. Instead she untied the ribbon again, right there at her bench, and unfolded the first letter from the beginning.

November 3rd, 1887

My dearest—

I have thought of nothing but Thursday since you left me. You must know this. You must feel it too, this thread that stretches between us even now, even as I write these words knowing you will not read them for days. I am yours across any distance. I am yours in the spaces between heartbeats.

You told me to be patient. I am trying. But patience is a discipline I have not yet mastered, not in this. Not when I can still feel where your hands rested at my waist. Not when I close my eyes and see you looking at me as you did when you dismissed me. That look. I have no words for that look except to say that I understood, in that moment, what it would mean to belong to someone entirely.

I have never belonged to anyone. I did not know I wanted to.

You have made me know.

Thursday cannot come soon enough.

Yours—entirely, always—

E.

Anna read it twice more before she reached for the next letter.

Her hands were not quite steady.

She reached for the next letter then set her hands flat on the bench.

* * *

She read them all, there in the empty workroom as the November dark came down outside the windows. Eighteen letters in total —she'd miscounted at first—spanning nearly two years, from November 1887 to September 1889. Most were in E.'s hand, but six were different: a smaller, more precise script on slightly cheaper paper. The dressmaker's responses, Anna realised. Kept, treasured, bundled together with E.'s own drafts or copies.

The picture emerged slowly, in fragments. E. was a woman of comfortable circumstances. Respectable. Unmarried, at least at first.

She attended dinners and concerts, paid calls, observed the rituals of her class. She was articulate, educated, prone to self-analysis.

And she was in love with her dressmaker.

Anna had to read three letters before she was certain. The references were oblique—necessarily so—but unmistakable once she knew what to look for. The fittings that lasted longer than fittings should. The way E. wrote about standing still, about waiting, about the particular quality of attention between them.

The dressmaker's letters were different. Where E. was effusive, spilling feeling across the page, the dressmaker was measured. Controlled. Her sentences were shorter, her declarations rarer, and when they came, they landed like stones dropped into still water.

You ask if I think of you, one of the dressmaker's letters read. *I think of little else. But thinking is not the same as speaking, and I have never been skilled at speaking. What I can do is show you. What I can do is wait for Thursday, and know that you will come to me, and trust that when you stand before me you will understand everything I cannot write.*

Be patient. I am teaching you something. You do not yet know what it is.

Anna set the letters down.

The workroom was fully dark now except for her bench lamp. It was fully dark now except for her bench lamp. She'd skipped lunch. She'd missed the last good hour of daylight. None of this moved her from the chair.

But she didn't move.

Be patient. I am teaching you something.

She thought about E. standing in a dressmaker's workshop, being measured, being fitted. Being *seen* in a way that had nothing to do with measurements. The dressmaker's hands on her, professional and not professional, and E. holding still because—

Because she'd been told to. Because holding still was what had been asked of her, and giving it felt like—

Anna didn't have a word for what it felt like. She kept seeing it—M.'s hand guiding Eleanor's posture, the fitting that was not a fitting—and her own body's response to the image would not quiet down.

She tidied the letters carefully, retied the ribbon, placed them back in the archival box. Tomorrow she would handle them properly. Take them to the reading room, document them, begin the process of formal assessment.

Tonight she went home through the wet streets, made tea she forgot to drink, and lay in bed staring at the ceiling while the rain tapped against her window.

I have never belonged to anyone. I did not know I wanted to.

The sentence kept circling back. She couldn't make it stop.

CHAPTER 2

Anna's flat was cold when she got home. The heating had been temperamental for weeks—she kept meaning to call the landlord, kept not doing it. Easier to wear an extra jumper than to make the phone call, arrange a time, be present for a stranger in her space.

She dropped her bag by the door and stood for a moment in the hallway, not turning on the lights. The streetlamp outside cast orange shadows through the front window. Sarah's room—not Sarah's room anymore, hadn't been for eight months—was dark behind its closed door. Anna hadn't opened it in weeks. There was no reason to. The bed was made, the shelves empty, the walls bare where Sarah's prints had hung.

She'd told herself she'd find another flatmate. Put up a notice, interview candidates, fill the silence with someone else's presence. But the months had slipped past, and somehow she'd never managed it. The flat was too quiet and she'd grown used to the quiet. That was the truth of it. Easier to be alone than to explain herself to someone new.

She made toast because she should eat something. Stood at the kitchen counter chewing mechanically, not tasting it. Her laptop was on the table where she'd left it that morning, and she thought about the transcriptions she'd started—just the first few letters, typed up quickly before Marcus had arrived. For cataloguing purposes.

Be patient. I am teaching you something.

Anna set down the toast.

There was a voicemail from her mother about Christmas that she'd been avoiding for three days. A shower she should take. A life she should probably attend to.

Instead she opened her laptop and pulled up the file.

She'd transcribed five letters so far. E.'s first three, and two of the dressmaker's. She read them again now, slowly, letting the words settle differently than they had in the workroom. There, under the fluorescent lights, with Marcus twenty feet away, the letters had felt like artifacts. Historical curiosities. Something to be processed and catalogued.

Here, alone in her dim kitchen, they felt like something else.

I have never belonged to anyone. I did not know I wanted to.

Anna closed the laptop. Left it closed for almost a minute.

She went to shower.

The bathroom mirror was fogged when she got out, and she wiped it clear without thinking, an automatic gesture. Her reflection looked back at her: pale skin, dark hair wet and tangled, the particular expression she always seemed to have lately. Tired. Watchful. Waiting for something she couldn't name.

Twenty-seven years old. She'd thought, at twenty-two, that by now she'd have figured something out. A relationship, at least. Something that lasted longer than a few months of awkwardness and apology. The boys at university had been fumbling and disappointing, and when she'd finally admitted to herself that the problem might not be the boys, the girls hadn't been much better. Different, yes. Closer to something. But still not right.

She'd started to think the problem was her.

Too much in her head. Too reserved. Unable to relax into the easy intimacy that seemed to come naturally to everyone else. Her last girlfriend—could she even call her that? Three months of dinners and films and sex that was fine, just fine, nothing wrong with it—had finally said, not unkindly, *I feel like you're somewhere else. Like you're waiting for something and I'm not it.*

Anna hadn't been able to argue. She hadn't known what she was waiting for. She only knew that she hadn't found it.

She wiped the mirror again, clearing the fresh fog. Looked at herself. Thin shoulders, small breasts, the body she'd always thought of as unremarkable. Serviceable. The kind of body that didn't draw attention, which had always suited her fine.

She thought about E., standing in the dressmaker's workshop. Being looked at. Being *seen.*

You stood so still for me, the dressmaker had written. Anna had read it three times in the workroom, that passage. *Three pins between my lips and my fingers at your seams and you waited as though waiting were the whole of your purpose.*

Without quite deciding to, Anna straightened her posture. Shoulders back. Chin level. The way you might stand if someone were measuring you. If someone were circling you slowly, assessing, taking note of every line and angle.

She watched herself in the mirror. The way her body changed when she held it like that—not dramatic, but present. Deliberate. A body being offered up for inspection.

Her face was flushed. She could see it in the glass.

She turned away, grabbed her towel, and went to the bedroom.

* * *

The transcription file was still open on her laptop. Anna sat on her bed in her pyjamas, laptop balanced on her knees, and told herself she was just reviewing her notes. Professional interest. The letters were genuinely significant—Victorian sapphic correspondence was rare enough, and this sustained, this intimate, potentially publishable if she handled it correctly.

She should be thinking about publication. About proper archival handling. About the career implications of a find like this.

She scrolled to the dressmaker's first letter.

November 10th, 1887

You ask if I think of you. You ask as though there were doubt. I wonder sometimes if you understand what you are, what you have already become to me. I suspect you do not. You came to me for a dress and did not know you were offering something else entirely.

I think of little else.

But thinking is not the same as speaking, and I have never been skilled at speaking. My hands know things my words cannot manage. What I can do is show you. What I can do is wait for Thursday, and know that you will come to me, and trust that when you stand before me you will understand everything I cannot write.

Be patient. I am teaching you something. You do not yet know what it is.

Yours—

M.

M. The dressmaker had a letter now. Anna lingered on it — one character doing the work of a whole woman. The way it looked at the bottom of the page, that single letter standing in for a whole woman.

She scrolled to the next letter. E.'s response, written four days later.

November 14th, 1887

I came home from you today and sat in my room for an hour without moving. Not because I was tired, though I was tired. Not because I was thinking, though I was thinking. Because you had not told me I could move, and some part of me was still waiting for permission.

Is that madness? It feels like madness. It feels like the sanest thing I have ever done.

You say I do not understand what I am becoming. You are right. I do not. I only know that before I met you I moved through the world like a guest in my own body, and now—now I am beginning to feel that I live there. That someone has given me the key.

Thursday was not enough. It is never enough. I stand in your workshop and time stops and then I leave and it begins again and everything between our Thursdays is just waiting. I am made of waiting, now. You have made me so.

Tell me what you want of me. Tell me and I will do it. I will do anything.

Yours—always, entirely—

E.

Anna's hand had drifted to her stomach. She noticed it now, her palm flat against her skin through the thin cotton of her pyjama top. Her breathing had changed—shallower, quicker.

She thought about closing the laptop. Going to sleep. Being sensible.

She scrolled to the next letter.

November 17th, 1887

You ask me to tell you what I want.

I want you to learn stillness. True stillness, not the performance of it. I want you to stand before me and let go of every impulse to speak, to move, to fill silence with yourself. I want you to trust me enough to be empty, and to let me fill you.

This is not about the body, though the body is where we begin. It is about surrender. You have spent your whole life being asked to perform— to be clever, to be charming, to be appropriate. I am asking you to stop. To give me the woman underneath all that. The one who does not know how to be still because no one has ever asked her to be.

I am asking.

Thursday. Wear the grey dress. Do not speak when you enter. Wait for me to address you.

M.

Anna read it again. Her hand had slipped beneath her waistband without her quite noticing—when had that happened? She was touching herself lightly, barely a brush of fingertips, but her body was already responding. Already wet. Already wanting something she couldn't articulate.

She thought about E. reading this letter. The grey dress. The instruction. *Do not speak when you enter.*

She thought about what it would feel like to walk into a room under those conditions. To have given away your voice before you even arrived. To stand in silence and wait—

Wait for me to address you.

Anna's fingers moved with more intention now. She let herself imagine it. Not E., not the dressmaker—something closer to herself. A room. A woman. Being looked at. Being assessed.

You may breathe.

The voice in her head was low, calm, certain. A voice that expected obedience because obedience was what had been offered. Anna's hips shifted against her hand. She was thinking about standing still. About being measured. About—

Tell me what you want of me.

—about giving someone permission to want things from her. About the specific relief of that. Of not having to know what she wanted, not having to perform desire correctly, just having to—

Be still. I am teaching you something.

She came with a gasp that surprised her, sudden and sharp, her body clenching around nothing. She pressed her face into the pillow and rode it out, shaking, her mind full of fragments: hands at her waist, a voice giving instructions, the particular quality of being seen.

Afterward she lay there with her heart pounding, laptop still open beside her, the dressmaker's words glowing on the screen.

I want you to trust me enough to be empty, and to let me fill you.

Anna stared at the ceiling.

She was twenty-seven years old and she had read thousands of letters and none of them had done this to her.

She lay there for a long time, and the sentence kept turning over in her mind, and she understood that she was not going to be able to put it down.

CHAPTER 3

The Bodleian's reading rooms had a quality of silence that Anna had always loved. There was always sound in it — pages turning, the creak of an old chair, footsteps somewhere in the stacks — but the room had a consistent hush that was as tangible as the building itself. Centuries of scholarship had soaked into these walls. The silence was a by-product of concentrated attention, generations of it, layered like sediment.

She had worked here for four years now. Conservation and preservation, the quiet work of keeping old things alive. Most days she loved it—the patience required, the detective work of identifying paper stocks and binding techniques, the satisfaction of stabilising a damaged spine or cleaning foxing from a title page. It suited her temperament: careful, methodical, more comfortable with objects than with people.

Today she sat at her usual desk in the Duke Humfrey's reading room, laptop open, surrounded by the materials she'd requested from the special collections. Victorian sexuality. Romantic friendship. The history of women's relationships before the categories hardened.

She was researching. That was the word for it. Research.

Three days had passed since she'd first read the letters, and she hadn't been able to think about anything else. She'd transcribed them all now—twelve from E., five from the dressmaker—working late into the night with a compulsion she didn't quite recognise in herself. The transcription file on her laptop had grown to twenty-three pages. She kept it open while she worked, kept glancing at it, kept finding her attention drifting from whatever she was supposed to be doing back to those familiar phrases.

I have never belonged to anyone. I did not know I wanted to.

The academic texts helped, in a way. They gave her distance. Sharon Marcus on female friendship in Victorian England. Martha Vicinus on intimate friends. Papers on romantic friendship, on Boston marriages, on the ways women had loved each other before there were words for it—or when the words that existed were too dangerous to use.

She learned that what E. and her dressmaker had was not unique, though it was rare to find it documented so explicitly. The Victorians had been more flexible about women's intimacy than she'd realised—provided it stayed within certain bounds, provided it could be read as sisterly affection or spiritual communion, it could hide in plain sight. The danger came when it became legible as something else. When the physical became undeniable. When someone named it.

The letters walked that line with extraordinary precision. E. wrote about standing still, about waiting, about the quality of attention between them—but rarely about bodies. The dressmaker wrote about instruction and obedience and surrender—but framed it in the language of craft, of fitting, of making a dress. Anyone reading casually might see only an unusually intense professional relationship. A gentlewoman uncommonly attached to her seamstress. Nothing actionable. Nothing that would ruin a reputation.

But Anna could read between the lines now. She understood what the silences meant. The fitting that lasted an entire afternoon. The dress that required adjustment after adjustment, appointment after appointment. The instruction that had nothing to do with cloth.

Be patient. I am teaching you something. You do not yet know what it is.

She found herself reading the same passages over and over. Not the tender ones, not the declarations of devotion—though those moved her too—but the ones about structure. About waiting. About the focused attention that E. described, the feeling of being held in place by nothing but expectation.

The academic literature had terms for this. Power exchange. Dominance and submission. She found them in footnotes, in tangential references, in the careful language of scholars who studied sexuality without quite inhabiting it. The words felt clinical, insufficient. They didn't capture what the letters captured—that sense of surrender as liberation, of obedience as intimacy, of being seen so completely that the seeing itself became a kind of touch.

She needed lunch. She needed to do something normal.

* * *

The staff canteen wasn't really a canteen—that word suggested fluorescent lights and steam trays, the institutional grimness of hospital cafeterias. This was something else: a high-ceilinged room in the old library building, stone walls softened by warm lighting, mismatched wooden tables that had probably been here since the 1950s. The university had renovated it five years ago, brought in a proper kitchen, hired actual chefs. Now it served the kind of food that academics could pretend was merely convenient while quietly appreciating that it was also good.

Anna came here most days. She told herself it was proximity —her workroom was just two buildings over—but the truth was she liked the atmosphere. The murmur of conversation, the smell of coffee, the way people nodded to her without requiring more than a nod in return. She could be alone in company here. It was the kind of solitude she preferred.

She collected her tray—roasted squash soup, bread that was still warm, an apple she probably wouldn't eat—and found her usual table by the window. From here she could see most of the room: the cluster of historians who always sat together by the door, the lone mathematicians scattered at individual tables with their laptops, the rotating cast of visiting researchers who looked slightly lost.

And the kitchen.

The serving area was semi-open, a long counter with the cooking happening just behind it, visible through a wide pass. Anna had never paid much attention to it before. Kitchens were kitchens. But today—

Today she noticed.

The woman running the line was perhaps thirty-five, dark hair pulled back. Not tall. As Anna watched, she said something to the younger cook beside her — Anna couldn't hear what — and he glanced up, said something back, and then went on doing what he was doing in a slightly different way. A few minutes later she leaned past him to taste something off his spoon, frowned, and reached for a jar without explaining herself. He waited until she'd finished, then started over.

Anna watched her taste something from a small spoon, frown slightly, add a pinch of something from a container by the stove. Watched her catch a server's eye and gesture toward a table where someone was waiting. Watched her wipe down a section of the counter with a cloth, a quick automatic motion, even as she was already turning to the next thing.

She'd seen this woman before. Of course she had—Anna ate here three or four times a week, had done for years. But she'd never really looked.

Now she was looking.

I want you to trust me enough to be empty, and to let me fill you.

Anna blinked. The dressmaker's words, rising unbidden. She looked down at her soup, her face warm.

This was ridiculous. She was sitting in a university canteen, eating lunch like a normal person, and her mind was—

She made herself take a spoonful of soup. It was good. Properly seasoned, the squash roasted until it caramelised, a hint of something warming underneath—ginger, maybe, or a touch of curry. Someone had taken care with this. Someone had paid attention.

When she looked up again, the woman in the kitchen was watching her.

It lasted only a moment. Eye contact across the room, brief and unremarkable—the chef scanning the dining area, noting who was eating, whether the food was disappearing from plates. Professional interest. Normal behaviour.

Anna looked away first. She didn't know why her heart was beating faster.

Back in the conservation workroom, she couldn't settle.

Marcus was at his bench, working on the herbal as always, earphones in, bobbing his head slightly to whatever he was listening to. Dr. Fitzwilliam had come through earlier to check on the Ashworth progress—Anna had shown her the standard materials, the household accounts and correspondence, mentioned the personal letters only briefly. "Romantic in nature," she'd said. "Potentially significant. I'm still assessing." Dr. Fitzwilliam had nodded and moved on, satisfied. There was no reason for anyone to look more closely.

Anna pulled up her transcription file. She'd meant to start on the condition reports for the rest of box seven—there was a collection of botanical drawings that needed cataloguing, a small notebook of household remedies—but instead she found herself scrolling through the letters again.

She noticed things she hadn't noticed before. The way the dressmaker's letters came less frequently than E.'s—one for every two or three of E.'s—but were longer when they came. The way E.'s handwriting changed over the course of the correspondence, becoming steadier, more controlled, as if the act of writing itself had become a discipline. The way certain phrases echoed between them, passed back and forth like a private language.

Yours—entirely, always. E. signed every letter this way. And the dressmaker, more simply: *Yours—M.*

M. Anna still didn't know her full name. The letters never used it. E. was probably Elizabeth, or Eleanor, or Emma—the Ashworth family records would tell her, if she looked. But M. was just M. A woman who made dresses, who gave instructions, who wrote with a precision that felt almost physical.

You ask what I thought when you stood before me for the first fitting. I will tell you, though I wonder if you are ready to hear it.

I thought: here is someone who does not know herself. Here is someone who has been performing for so long that she has forgotten there might be something underneath the performance. And I thought: I would like to find out what is there. I would like to strip away the layers—not of cloth, though that too—and see what remains when there is nothing left to hide behind.

This is not a kind thought. I know that. There is a selfishness in it, a hunger. I wanted to take you apart and see how you were made. I still want this. I suspect I will always want this.

But here is the thing I did not expect: I also wanted to put you back together. Differently. Better. I wanted to remake you into something that knew its own worth. That could stand still not because it was afraid to move, but because stillness was chosen. Offered. Given.

I do not know if I am capable of this. I only know that when you are with me, I want to try.

Anna realised her hand was pressed flat against her chest, as if to hold something in.

I wanted to take you apart and see how you were made.

She thought about the chef in the canteen. The quick, sure hands. The way the staff around her responded to her presence. The brief moment of eye contact across the room.

This was absurd. She didn't know this woman at all. She'd never spoken to her, didn't know her name, had no reason to think—

But that was the thing. She was noticing now, in a way she never had before. The letters had given her a lens, and suddenly the world looked different through it. The dynamics she'd always filtered out were becoming visible. The small negotiations of authority and deference that happened everywhere, all the time, between people who probably didn't even know they were doing it.

Her colleague James, asking Dr. Fitzwilliam's permission before moving a crate of materials. The way he ducked his head slightly, waited for her nod. The new archivist, Sophie, watching the senior staff for cues about where to sit, how to speak, when to ask questions. The junior cook in the canteen, adjusting his technique the moment the chef touched his elbow.

It was everywhere. It had always been everywhere. Anna just hadn't had the vocabulary to see it.

Now she did.

* * *

She went back to the canteen for tea at four o'clock. She often got tea in the afternoon. If she checked her hair in the toilets first, and took a table with a clearer view of the kitchen, those were small adjustments she did not need to account for to anyone, including herself.

The chef was still there. Of course she was—the kitchen served until five, and someone had to run it. She'd changed into a fresh apron since lunch, Anna noticed. Her sleeves were rolled up, forearms bare, and there was a small burn mark on the inside of her left wrist that looked old, healed over. An occupational hazard.

Anna collected her tea and sat down. She had a book with her —one of the academic texts, Martha Vicinus, because she wasn't quite ready to give up the pretence that this was research—and she opened it to a random page and did not read a single word.

The kitchen was quieter now. The lunch rush was long over, and only a handful of people sat in the dining room, mostly lingering over coffee and laptops. The chef was doing something with inventory, Anna thought—checking supplies, making notes on a clipboard, moving between the storage area and the counter with the systematic attention of someone who knew exactly what needed doing and in what order.

At one point she stood on tiptoe, looking at something on a high shelf, then asked the younger cook to fetch the step stool. He brought it. She climbed up, reached, swore quietly when whatever she wanted turned out to be further back than she'd thought, and had to brace one hand on the shelf to drag it forward. When she came down she was holding a small paper bag and was already talking to the cook about something else.

Anna watched the whole exchange with an attention that felt almost indecent. The small request, casually given. The immediate compliance. The nod of approval.

Her tea was going cold. She should drink it. She should read her book. She should do something other than stare at a woman she'd never met and project an entire fantasy onto the way she ran her kitchen.

But she couldn't stop seeing it. The shape of something she recognised, now that she knew what to look for. Not the same as the letters—nothing so formal, so ritualised—but something in the same family. A woman who was comfortable with authority. Who wielded it easily, without cruelty, with the expectation that it would be respected.

Anna wondered what it would feel like to work for her. To be the one receiving those small corrections, those brief nods of approval. To know exactly what was expected and to feel the quiet satisfaction of meeting that expectation.

She closed her book. She'd read the same paragraph four times without absorbing a word of it.

But when she stood to leave, she glanced toward the kitchen one more time, and the chef was watching her again. This time the look lasted a moment longer—long enough to be a look, not just a glance. Long enough for Anna to feel seen.

Then the chef turned back to her work, and Anna walked out of the canteen on legs that felt slightly unreliable, and told herself that it didn't mean anything, it couldn't mean anything, she was projecting, she was building a fantasy from fragments the way E. must have done before that first fitting, before she knew what she was walking into—

I have never belonged to anyone. I did not know I wanted to.

Anna went home and did not sleep well.

* * *

The next morning, she arrived at work early.

The workroom was empty—Marcus wouldn't be in for another hour, and Dr. Fitzwilliam rarely appeared before ten. Anna had the space to herself, the familiar smell of old paper and conservation adhesive, the grey November light filtering through the high windows.

She sat at her bench and opened her laptop, but instead of the transcription file, she opened a browser. She typed slowly, as if the words might judge her: *power exchange relationships.*

The results were overwhelming. Thousands of pages, forums, articles, academic papers and personal blogs and everything in between. Anna scrolled through them with the same systematic attention she brought to provenance research, clicking on links, reading quickly, building a framework.

She learned words she hadn't known. Dominant and submissive, obviously, but also: negotiation. Consent. Limits, hard and soft. Aftercare. Scene. The vocabulary of a subculture that had been developing its own language for decades, maybe longer, while she'd been entirely unaware of its existence.

Some of what she found made her uncomfortable—the imagery was often harsh, the dynamics more extreme than anything in the letters. But underneath the surface variations, she kept recognising the same essential shape. The same exchange that M. had written about so carefully: power given, power received. The intimacy of trusting someone enough to surrender.

She found forums where people discussed their relationships with a frankness that astonished her. Women who had been doing this for years. Who talked about their dynamics the way other people talked about marriage or dating—practically, affectionately, with the casual expertise of lived experience.

One thread caught her attention. Someone asking for advice: they'd discovered this part of themselves late, in their thirties, and didn't know how to reconcile it with the life they'd already built. The responses were what internet responses tended to be. Two people wrote at length about their own discoveries, which sounded nothing like the original poster's. One person told her she should have known sooner. Someone recommended a podcast. Near the bottom, in a single line, a stranger had written: *you don't have to do anything with it yet, you can just know it.*

Anna read that one a few times, mostly because she wasn't sure she agreed.

She thought about E., a respectable Victorian gentlewoman, walking into a dressmaker's shop and walking out changed. About the years of fittings that followed, the slow unfolding of whatever had begun in that first meeting. E. hadn't known either, at first. She hadn't had the vocabulary or the framework. She'd only had the dressmaker, and the letters, and the willingness to discover something about herself she hadn't known was there.

Anna closed her browser. The workroom was still empty. Outside the window, a grey sky was threatening rain.

She did not feel awake, exactly. She felt the way she imagined people felt when they realised they had been wearing the wrong prescription for years.

CHAPTER 4

The Ashworth bequest inventory was a forty-three-page document typed on a manual typewriter sometime in the 1970s, full of abbreviations and cross-references that required a decoder ring to parse. Anna had been avoiding it—there was enough work in the boxes themselves without wrestling with the paperwork—but this morning she'd arrived early again, unable to sleep past five, and the inventory had seemed like a reasonable way to occupy herself until Marcus arrived.

She was on page twenty-six when she found it.

Textile collection (Ashworth, E.M.), donated 1962, transferred to Costume & Textile storage. See separate catalogue ref. CT/1962/14.

Anna read it twice. Then a third time.

E.M. Ashworth. The initials matched the signature on the letters—*Yours—entirely, always—E.* The bequest she'd been processing was the family collection, donated after the last Ashworth died in 2019. But this was something else. A separate donation, decades earlier. Textiles.

Dresses.

Her hands were not quite steady as she pulled up the university's collections database. The system was old, clunky, designed in an era when nobody imagined researchers might want to search across departments. She typed in the catalogue reference. The system took its time.

CT/1962/14: Ashworth textile collection. 47 items. Women's clothing, accessories, and household textiles, circa 1870-1920. Donor: Estate of Eleanor Mary Ashworth (1857-1943). Condition: variable. Location: Textile Repository, Banbury Road.

Eleanor Mary Ashworth. 1857-1943.

E.

Anna sat back in her chair. The workroom was silent around her—Marcus wouldn't arrive for another forty minutes—and she could hear her own breathing, slightly too fast. Eleanor. She had a name now. A birth year, a death year, a life that had spanned nearly a century. A woman who had written those letters at thirty, who had stood in a dressmaker's workshop learning stillness, who had kept those letters her entire life and then—what? Donated her clothing to a university? Had someone else done that, after she died? A relative clearing out an old woman's wardrobe, not knowing what any of it meant?

Forty-seven items. Variable condition. Somewhere in a storage facility on Banbury Road.

The dress might be there.

Anna's mind was racing. The letters mentioned a dress—*the dress*—several times, though she hadn't focused on those passages yet. Something about alterations. Something about wearing it in company. She pulled up her transcription file, scrolling quickly, searching for the references she half-remembered.

There. January 1888, one of M.'s letters:

The green silk is nearly finished. I have made the modifications we discussed—you will feel them when you wear it, though no one else will see. The boning along the left seam will press just slightly with each breath. A reminder. You asked me once how you could carry our Thursdays with you into the rest of your week. This is my answer. You will sit at dinner with your family and feel my work against your ribs, and you will know that even there, even among all those people who do not see you as I see you, you are still mine.

Anna's throat was tight.

She thought about Eleanor—she had a name now, she could think of her by name—sitting at a family dinner in 1888, wearing a dress that no one else understood. Hidden in plain sight. The submission built into the seams, the obedience pressed against her body with every breath. A secret shared across a room full of people who had no idea what they were looking at.

The green silk.

It might still exist. Forty-seven items in a textile repository, poorly catalogued, donated over sixty years ago. Nobody had looked at them properly in decades, probably. Nobody had known what to look for.

Anna opened the research request form. Her fingers hesitated over the keyboard. She needed a reason—a legitimate scholarly reason to access a collection outside her department. Conservation assessment? No, that wasn't her remit for external collections. Cross-referencing with the Ashworth papers? Closer, but she'd need to explain what she was cross-referencing.

She typed: *Research request: CT/1962/14 (Ashworth textile collection). Purpose: Provenance research in connection with recently catalogued Ashworth correspondence (Bodleian, Ashworth bequest 2019). Specific interest: garments referenced in correspondence, potential for material culture analysis. Requesting access for visual examination and condition assessment.*

It was thin, but it would do. Conservators requested cross-departmental access all the time. Nobody would question it.

She submitted the form before she could second-guess herself.

* * *

The morning passed in a blur. Anna went through the motions of her work—condition reports, provenance notes, the careful handling of old paper—but her mind was elsewhere. Two elsewheres, really. The textile repository on Banbury Road, where forty-seven items waited in climate-controlled storage. And the canteen, where lunch service would start in an hour.

She told herself the two fixations were unrelated. The dress was historical research, a legitimate extension of her work on the letters. The chef was—

The chef was something else.

At half past twelve, Anna saved her work, closed her laptop, and walked to the canteen. She didn't check her hair this time. She didn't adjust her clothes or rehearse conversation openers or do any of the things she might have done if she'd admitted to herself what she was doing. She just walked, and arrived, and collected a tray with soup and bread and an apple she wouldn't eat, and found a table with a clear view of the kitchen.

The chef was there.

Of course she was there—it was lunch service, where else would she be?—but Anna felt something settle in her chest at the sight of her. The dark hair pulled back. The quick, certain hands. The way she moved through the kitchen like she owned it, because she did, because it was hers.

Today Anna didn't pretend to read. She didn't pull out a book or her phone or any of the props she usually used to justify her presence. She just sat, and ate her soup slowly, and watched.

The lunch rush was in full swing. The chef worked the line with her two assistants, plating dishes, checking temperatures, keeping the rhythm steady. Anna watched her taste something from a spoon, add a pinch of salt, taste again. Watched her catch a server's eye with a small nod that meant *this one's ready*. Watched her touch the younger cook's shoulder—a brief correction, redirecting his attention—and then move on without waiting to see if he'd comply. He did, of course. Everyone did.

The chef looked up.

Their eyes met across the dining room. Anna didn't look away.

She should have. She knew she should have—it was too obvious, too exposed, sitting here staring at a woman she'd never spoken to like she was trying to memorise her. The letters, the research, the dress waiting in its storage facility. She felt reckless in a way she didn't recognise. Like Eleanor must have felt, walking into that dressmaker's shop for the first time, not knowing what she was walking into but knowing it was going to change her.

The chef held her gaze for a long moment. Then the corner of her mouth twitched—amused, maybe, or confirming something to herself—and she turned back to her work.

She looked down at her soup, which had gone cold, and made herself take a spoonful. Her heart was pounding so hard she could feel it in her throat.

She stayed anyway. Finished her soup, or most of it. Watched the lunch rush wind down, the dining room emptying as people returned to their offices and libraries. The kitchen shifted into a different register—clean-up, prep for the afternoon, the slower rhythm of non-service hours. The chef disappeared into the back for a few minutes, then re-emerged without her apron, sleeves still rolled up, checking something on a clipboard.

Anna should leave. She had work to do. The afternoon was half gone already, and she hadn't finished the condition reports from this morning, and there was no reason to sit here in an emptying canteen like someone waiting for—

The chef was walking toward her.

Not toward the dining room in general, not toward another table, but toward her, specifically, with a directness that made Anna's mouth go dry. She was smiling now—a real smile, easy and a little amused—and she moved the way she did everything, with the unhurried confidence of someone who expected the world to arrange itself around her.

"You're the one who fixes old books, right?"

Her voice was warm. Lower than Anna had expected, with a hint of an accent she couldn't quite place. Manchester, maybe, softened by years in the south.

"I—yes." Anna's own voice came out slightly strangled. She cleared her throat. "Conservation. I work in conservation."

"Conservation." The chef said the word like she was tasting it, testing its weight. "That's the one where you fix the bindings and clean the pages and all that?"

"More or less. It's—there's more to it than that, but yes. Essentially."

"I've seen you around." The chef pulled out the chair across from Anna and sat down, easy as anything, like they'd arranged to meet here. "You come in most days. Soup, bread, apple you never eat. Always sit by the window."

She'd thought she was invisible. Apparently she'd been wrong about that too.

"I like the light," she managed. "By the window. It's—the light is good."

The chef's smile widened. "The light. Right." She extended her hand across the table. "I'm Margot."

"Anna." Her hand was in Margot's before she'd consciously decided to move it. The grip was firm, warm, callused in places from years of kitchen work. "I'm Anna."

"I know." Margot released her hand but didn't lean back, didn't create distance. "I asked around. The quiet conservator who reads academic books at lunch and watches my kitchen like she's taking notes." A beat. "Are you? Taking notes?"

Anna's brain short-circuited. She opened her mouth, closed it, opened it again. "I—no. I wasn't—I mean, I was just—"

"Relax." Margot's voice was gentle, teasing but not cruel. "I'm not accusing you of anything. I was just curious. You've got this way of watching. Very focused. Like you're trying to figure something out."

Anna didn't know what to say to that. It was too close to the truth—she *had* been trying to figure something out, something she barely had language for, and Margot's kitchen had become part of the puzzle. But she couldn't explain that. She couldn't explain any of it.

"I like watching people who are good at things," she said finally. It came out more honest than she'd intended. "You're good at what you do. It's—interesting. To watch."

Something shifted in Margot's expression. The teasing warmth was still there, but underneath it, a flicker of something else. Interest, maybe. Recognition.

"You think so?"

"Yes." Anna was on firmer ground now, talking about observable facts rather than her own incomprehensible feelings. "The way you run your kitchen. Everyone knows exactly what they're supposed to do, and they do it. You don't have to repeat yourself or raise your voice. You just—" She gestured vaguely, trying to capture it. "You expect things, and they happen."

Margot was quiet for a moment, studying Anna with an attention that felt almost physical. Then she laughed—a real laugh, surprised and pleased.

"That's the nicest thing anyone's said about my management style. Usually people just complain about the hours." She leaned back in her chair, but her eyes stayed on Anna's face. "Conservation, though. That's got to be interesting. All those old books, all that history. You must find some wild stuff."

Anna thought about the letters. About Eleanor and M. and the green silk dress that might be sitting in a storage facility right now, waiting to be found.

"Sometimes," she said. "Sometimes you find things you weren't expecting."

"Yeah?" Margot tilted her head. "Like what?"

Anna hesitated. She barely knew this woman. She shouldn't—

"Letters," she heard herself say. "I found some letters recently. Victorian. They're—" She stopped, not sure how to continue. "They're not what I expected."

"Letters." Margot's eyebrows rose. "What kind of letters?"

"Love letters." The words were out before Anna could stop them. "Between two women. Very—intimate. I'm still trying to understand them, I think."

She didn't know why she'd said that. Any of it. This was a stranger, a woman she'd spoken to for all of three minutes, and Anna was telling her about the letters she'd barely told anyone, the letters that had cracked open something inside her she was still trying to name.

But Margot didn't look shocked or uncomfortable. She looked interested. Genuinely, attentively interested.

"Victorian lesbian love letters," she said. "In the university archives. That's amazing. Does anyone else know about them?"

"Not really. I've flagged them for the special collections librarian, but I haven't—I'm still assessing them. Figuring out what they are."

"And what are they?"

Anna met Margot's eyes. The dining room was almost empty now. The afternoon light was slanting through the windows, catching dust motes, turning everything golden and strange.

"I don't know yet," she said. "But I think they're important. To me, anyway."

Margot held her gaze for a long moment. Then she nodded, once, like Anna had passed some kind of test.

"I'd like to hear more about them sometime," she said. "If you wanted to tell me." She pulled her phone from her back pocket, checked the time, grimaced. "I've got to get back—prep for tomorrow doesn't do itself. But look, there's this coffee place on Little Clarendon Street. Turl Street Kitchen. You know it?"

Anna nodded, mute.

"I'm off Saturday afternoon. If you wanted to get coffee. Talk about your letters, or whatever." Margot stood, pushed her chair back under the table. "No pressure. But I think you're interesting, Anna who fixes old books. And I'd like to know what you're figuring out."

She was leaving. She was actually leaving, walking back toward the kitchen, and Anna's mouth opened before her brain caught up.

"Yes."

Margot turned back, eyebrows raised.

"Saturday," Anna said. "Coffee. Yes. I'd—yes."

Margot's smile was slow and warm and did something complicated to Anna's chest.

"Saturday, then. Two o'clock?"

"Two o'clock."

"Good." Margot's eyes held hers for one more moment. "I'll see you then, Anna."

And then she was gone, back through the kitchen doors, and Anna was sitting alone at her table by the window with her cold soup and her uneaten apple and a feeling in her chest like something had just begun.

* * *

She floated back to the workroom.

There was no other word for it. She walked the familiar route—across the quad, through the corridor, up the stairs—but she barely registered any of it. Her body was on autopilot while her mind replayed the conversation on a loop. Margot's voice. Margot's smile. The way Margot had looked at her when she'd talked about the letters, like Anna was saying something that mattered.

I think you're interesting, Anna who fixes old books.

Nobody had ever called her interesting before. Quiet, yes. Clever, occasionally. Good at her job, when her supervisors remembered to notice. But interesting implied something else—something worth paying attention to, worth pursuing.

Margot had pursued her. Had asked around, learned her name, noticed her habits. Had walked across a dining room to talk to her, casual as anything, like it was the most natural thing in the world.

Anna sat down at her bench and opened her laptop. She should work. She should finish the condition reports, check on her research request, do any of the hundred things that constituted her actual job. Instead she stared at the screen and thought about Saturday.

Two days away. Two days to figure out what she was going to say, how she was going to explain herself, whether she was going to tell Margot more about the letters or keep them safely theoretical. Two days to decide if this was a date or just coffee, if Margot's interest was romantic or merely friendly, if Anna even knew the difference anymore.

Her email pinged. She clicked over to it automatically, grateful for the distraction.

RE: Research request CT/1962/14

Anna's heart stuttered.

Dear Ms. Levine,

Your request to access the Ashworth textile collection has been approved. The collection is currently housed in our Banbury Road facility and can be made available for examination at your convenience. Please contact the textile repository directly to arrange a viewing time.

Best regards,

Dr. Helena Cross

Curator, Costume and Textile Collections

Anna read the email three times.

Approved. The request had been approved. She could go to Banbury Road, could open those boxes that had been sitting untouched for decades, could look for the green silk dress that M. had altered with hidden boning and secret weight—

She had a green silk dress to find. And on Saturday, she had coffee.

Anna closed her eyes. The workroom hummed quietly around her—Marcus's music leaking faintly from his earphones, the heating system clicking, the ancient building settling into itself. She could hear Marcus's music leaking from his earphones and the heating system clicking and none of it had anything to do with where her mind had gone.

She thought about Eleanor, a hundred and thirty years ago, walking into a dressmaker's shop for an ordinary fitting and walking out changed. Had it felt like this? This sense of standing at a threshold, knowing that if you stepped through, nothing would be the same?

I have never belonged to anyone. I did not know I wanted to.

Anna opened her laptop and began composing an email to the textile repository. She had a green silk dress to find.

And on Saturday, she had coffee.

CHAPTER 5

Anna changed three times before leaving her flat.

The first outfit was a blouse she wore to conferences, buttoned to the collar—she looked like she was about to deliver a paper on sixteenth-century binding techniques. The second was a jumper with a small hole near the hem. The third was a grey cardigan over a white top, dark jeans, the silver earrings her mother had given her two birthdays ago. She looked, she decided, like she hadn't been thinking about this since Wednesday. Good enough.

Turl Street Kitchen was a ten-minute walk. She arrived twelve minutes early and stood outside for eight of them, pretending to check her phone, before pushing through the door at four to two.

Margot was at a table by the window with a book and a cup of something hot. Out of her kitchen whites she looked different— green jumper, hair loose around her shoulders—but the steadiness was the same. She read the way she cooked: with her full attention, like the book might try to get away if she let up.

She looked up as Anna approached. "You came."

"I said I would."

"You did." Margot closed her book—a battered French paper-back—and gestured to the opposite chair. "But people say things. I wasn't sure if you were the kind who meant them."

Anna sat, tucking her bag under the table. "I usually mean what I say. I just don't usually say very much."

"I noticed. Three months of watching you eat lunch and I think I heard you speak maybe twice. Both times to ask for extra bread."

"Your bread is very good."

"It is." No false modesty—just agreement. "I'll tell David. He gets in at five every morning to start the dough. He'll be pleased someone noticed."

A young server appeared, clearly new, holding his notepad like a shield. "Can I get you something?"

Anna opened her mouth to order and Margot said, "She'll have the oat milk latte. And one of the almond pastries." She looked at Anna. "Trust me?"

It was such a small thing. Ordering for her. Deciding what she'd drink. Anna felt it land somewhere below her ribs, warm and specific.

"That sounds fine," she said.

The server left. Margot watched him go. "Started last week. He'll get there, but right now he's moving at the wrong speed—too fast when he should wait, too slow when it counts."

Anna filed the observation away alongside everything else she'd been collecting: the nod of approval at the canteen, the one-word corrections, the way a kitchen full of people moved to Margot's rhythm without apparent effort.

"So," Margot said. "Conservation. Tell me what that actually means. Not the elevator version. The real thing."

Nobody asked about the actual work. People wanted the interesting finds, the old books. Nobody cared about adhesive testing or paper stock identification.

"It's methodical," Anna said, feeling her way. "Mostly assessment. You get a book or a manuscript and before you do anything, you have to understand the physical object. The paper, the binding, the kind of damage and how it happened."

"So you're reading the thing before you read the text."

"Exactly." Something loosened in Anna's chest—the relief of being understood quickly. "The text is almost secondary. My job is the object itself. How it was made, how it's aged, how to stop it from aging further."

"And you can tell all that by looking?"

"Looking. Touching. Sometimes smelling—different kinds of decay have different signatures." She paused, then said what she actually meant: "It's intimate, in a way. You spend hours with something. You learn it. You see where hands have touched it, where someone revised or reconsidered. You end up knowing it better than the people who made it."

"Intimate." Margot turned the word over. "I think about food that way. You make something with your hands and then someone puts it in their body. Takes it apart, absorbs it. That's intimate too."

The coffees arrived. The server set them down with visible concentration, trying to get it right. Margot gave him a small nod and he retreated looking steadier.

Anna wrapped her hands around the cup. The latte was good. She didn't know why she'd expected otherwise.

"How did you end up running a university kitchen?" she asked. "It seems like you could be somewhere bigger."

Margot laughed. "Bigger isn't better. I've worked bigger kitchens—restaurants in Manchester, a stretch in London that nearly killed me. The hours, the pressure. I was good at it and I was miserable." She shrugged. "Came here eight years ago for what was meant to be temporary. Needed out of London, knew someone who knew someone. And then I just stayed. The work is good. I have time to read. To have a life."

"To have coffee on Saturday afternoons."

"To have coffee on Saturday afternoons." Margot's eyes met hers across the table. "With women who watch my kitchen and won't tell me why."

Anna's stomach dropped—the good kind of drop, the kind that means you've been caught and part of you wanted to be. "I told you why. You're good at what you do."

"You told me you like watching people who are good at things. That's not the same as why you were watching *me*."

The question sat between them. Anna could deflect. She'd done it with everyone who'd tried to get close—the polite retreat, the change of subject, the thousand small withdrawals that made it easier to be alone. She'd been doing it so long she barely noticed anymore.

Margot waited. She was good at waiting.

"I was trying to understand something," Anna said. "Something I read in the letters. About dynamics. The way people relate to each other when one person is in charge and the other—"

"Isn't?"

"Isn't. Or is, but differently. I don't have the right words for it yet."

"I think you have more words than you're letting yourself use. You can say what you mean, Anna. I won't be shocked."

Anna took a breath. "The letters I found. The Victorian ones. They're not just love letters. The woman who wrote them was involved with her dressmaker, and there was a structure between them. One of them gave instructions and the other—" she could feel the heat in her face and pushed through it—"the other wanted to follow them. Wanted to be told. And I'd never read anything like it before, I'd never even thought about it, but when I read those letters I—"

She stopped. Margot had gone very still.

"You recognised something," Margot said.

"Yes." Barely a whisper. "I recognised something."

The café went on around them. The espresso machine, the clatter of cups, someone laughing at a table near the door. Anna had just said more to a near-stranger than she'd said to anyone in her life, and the world hadn't ended. It was just Saturday. People were drinking coffee.

"And you were watching me," Margot said, "because of how I run my kitchen."

Anna nodded.

"Because I'm in charge. Because people do what I say."

Another nod.

Margot exhaled—almost a laugh, not quite. "Well. That's more interesting than 'I like your soup.'"

Anna looked up. Margot was smiling, warm and unsurprised, like Anna had confirmed something she'd already guessed.

"I like your soup too," Anna said. "For what it's worth."

Now Margot really laughed, and the knot in Anna's chest came loose. "Good to know. I'll tell the team." She leaned forward, elbows on the table. "Can I ask you something?"

"Yes."

"Have you explored this? The dynamic you're describing? With anyone?"

Anna shook her head. "I didn't know it was a thing to explore. Until the letters. I just thought—" She stopped.

"Thought what?"

"That I was bad at relationships. That I couldn't connect properly. Every time I tried—boys at university, then women—it never felt right. I was always waiting for something and I didn't know what. I thought the problem was me."

"And now?"

Anna met her eyes. "Now I think the problem was that I didn't know what I needed."

Margot studied her for a long moment. Then she reached across the table and covered Anna's hand with her own. Warm. Callused. Steady.

"That's brave," she said. "Figuring that out. Saying it to someone you barely know."

"I don't feel brave. I feel terrified."

"Both things can be true at once." Margot's thumb moved once across the back of Anna's hand, then she withdrew it—deliberately, Anna thought. Drawing a line. "I'm going to be honest with you, because I think you'd rather have honesty than comfort."

Anna nodded.

"I've done this. What you're describing. I've been on the other side of it—the giving side, if you want to call it that. Not with everyone, not all the time, but when it fits." Her gaze was level, unhurried. "I noticed you before you started noticing me. The way you came into the canteen and tried to take up as little space as possible. The way you watched people. I thought: she doesn't know what she's looking for yet. And then you started watching me, and I thought—maybe she's working it out."

Anna's breath had gone shallow. "And now?"

"Now I think I was right." Margot leaned back. The hand was gone; the space between them felt wider. "But you're at the beginning of something, and I won't rush you. So we're going to finish our coffee, and I'm going to ask you about your letters, and then I'll walk you home and say goodnight. If you want to do this again, you've got my number."

Anna sat with the mixture of relief and disappointment—and underneath both, the unfamiliar comfort of someone else drawing the boundary. Of not having to decide.

"Okay," she said. "Tell me about the book you were reading when I came in."

And Margot did. The French paperback was Annie Ernaux, *La Place*—about class and memory and the gap between the life you came from and the one you built. Margot talked about it the way she talked about food, with precision and care, and Anna listened and asked questions and discovered that she was genuinely interested, that the attraction wasn't just the kitchen authority and the steady hands but the mind behind them.

They talked for another hour. The light through the windows went from gold to amber. Anna ate her almond pastry, which was excellent—Margot had chosen well, which Anna noted and filed away with everything else. She told Margot about Eleanor's full name, about the textile repository, about the green silk dress that might be sitting on a shelf on Banbury Road. Margot listened closely and asked questions that proved she'd been paying attention.

"I hope you find it," she said. "The dress."

"Me too."

They walked back to Anna's flat as the light faded. Margot kept pace beside her, not touching, near enough that Anna was conscious of the space between them—its precise width, its refusal to close.

At the door to her building, they stopped.

"Thank you," Anna said. "For the coffee. For listening."

"Thank you for telling me what you told me. That takes trust. We've known each other about three hours."

"It felt safe," Anna said. "Telling you."

"Good." Margot stepped closer. Anna's breath caught—but instead of kissing her, Margot touched her arm. A brief grip, just above the elbow, firm through the wool of her cardigan. Then she let go.

"Goodnight, Anna. Read your letters. Find your dress. Text me if you want to do this again."

"I will. I want to."

Margot smiled. "Then I'll hear from you."

She walked back the way they'd come, and Anna stood on her doorstep with her keys in her hand and the pressure of that grip still registering on her arm.

* * *

Inside, she dropped her bag and walked to her bedroom without turning on any lights. Sat on the edge of her bed. The streetlamp outside laid orange bars across the duvet.

She kept thinking about Margot's hand over hers at the café. The calluses. The deliberate way she'd withdrawn it—I won't rush you —setting a boundary Anna hadn't asked for but had needed.

Anna pulled off her cardigan. Then her jeans. She lay back in her underwear and put her hands on her stomach and breathed and tried to think about something else and failed.

She thought about Eleanor at her first fitting. The letters never described that moment directly—they started later, after the shape of the relationship had already set—but Anna could construct it from what came after. The respectable woman standing on a low platform. The dressmaker circling her with a measuring tape and a mouthful of pins, looking at Eleanor's body the way she looked at fabric: assessing the material, seeing what it could become.

When Anna tried to picture the dressmaker now, the image wouldn't stay. The dark hair, the working hands—they kept resolving into Margot.

She let them.

In her mind she stood in the middle of a room that belonged to no particular place. She wore something thin. Margot walked slowly around her, not touching, just looking—the same focused scrutiny Anna had watched her turn on a sauce that wasn't right, on a cook whose knife angle was off, on a plate that needed one more adjustment before it could leave the pass.

Anna's hand moved between her legs. She was already wet.

"Your posture's wrong," said the Margot in her head. Low, calm, factual. "Straighten your spine."

Anna straightened. On the bed, her back pressed flat against the mattress.

"Shoulders back. Not that far. There."

In the fantasy, Margot's hand corrected the small of her back— not gentle, not rough. Practical. The same touch she used to redirect a cook's grip on a pan handle.

"Chin up. Look at me."

Anna looked. Margot's eyes saw everything. That was the whole point—being looked at by someone who knew what she was seeing.

"Good."

The word hit her like a physical thing. Stomach, chest, lower.

The fantasy cut forward the way fantasies do—past logistics, past transitions. Margot behind her now. One hand flat on Anna's belly, holding her still. The other inside her, two fingers, steady. Not fast. A rhythm that didn't negotiate.

"I didn't say you could move."

Anna stayed still. In the fantasy, held. On her bed, every muscle taut, her hips trying to push into her own hand and her mind pulling them back. The restraint was the point. Having nothing to decide, nothing to perform. Just the instruction and the following of it.

She came hard and sudden, gasping into the empty room, and didn't muffle it.

Afterward she lay in the dark with her heart going and the fantasy dissolving around her—Margot's voice fading, the imagined room collapsing back into the ordinary shapes of her bedroom. The streetlamp. The Saturday-night traffic.

She was alone. She'd been alone for a long time. But tonight the aloneness had a different quality. Not absence—intermission. A space between what had just happened and what might happen next.

She reached for her phone.

Thank you again for today. I'd like to do it again. Whenever you're free.

She sent it before she could talk herself out of it.

Three minutes. Then:

Dinner next week? My place. I'll cook.

Anna typed *Yes* and sent it and set the phone down and pulled the covers up and lay there in the dark, thinking about Margot's hand on her arm, thinking about Eleanor's green silk dress, thinking about a Thursday in 1887 when a woman walked into a workshop and the rest of her life started.

She fell asleep still turning it over. Not a revelation. Just the feeling of a door she'd walked past a thousand times, and had finally tried the handle, and it had opened.

CHAPTER 6

The textile repository was a low brick building on Banbury Road, tucked between a dental practice and a solicitor's office. Anna had walked past it dozens of times without ever noticing it—the kind of building that seemed designed to be overlooked, its purpose announced only by a small brass plaque beside the door: *University Collections Storage. Authorised Personnel Only.*

Inside, it smelled of climate control and archival boxes. The reception area was small, functional, staffed by a grey-haired woman who examined Anna's credentials with the careful suspicion of someone who had spent decades protecting old things from well-meaning academics.

"Ashworth collection," she said, checking Anna's paperwork against something on her computer. "CT/1962/14. You're the first person to request access in—" she scrolled, squinting "—seventeen years."

"That long?"

"Textiles aren't fashionable. Pardon the pun." The woman's expression suggested she did not, in fact, pardon it. "Most researchers want the medieval manuscripts or the early printed books. Nobody cares about Victorian dresses anymore."

"I do," Anna said.

The woman looked at her for a moment—really looked, as if reassessing. Then she nodded and stood. "Follow me."

They went through a security door, down a long corridor, and into a room that was smaller than Anna had expected. Metal shelving lined three walls, stacked with acid-free boxes in various sizes. A large examination table occupied the centre, covered with clean white cotton. The lighting was excellent—bright but diffused, designed to show detail without causing damage.

"The Ashworth materials are on the far wall," the woman said, gesturing. "Forty-seven items, as listed. Gloves are in the drawer there. Don't remove anything from the boxes without support—the fabrics are fragile. If you need assistance, there's a bell by the door."

"Thank you."

The woman paused at the threshold. "Seventeen years," she said again. "Whatever you're looking for, I hope it's still there."

Then she was gone, and Anna was alone with forty-seven boxes that might or might not contain a green silk dress with hidden alterations, made by a dressmaker whose name she still didn't know, for a woman named Eleanor who had died eighty years ago.

She pulled on the cotton gloves and got to work.

* * *

The first box contained undergarments. Chemises, petticoats, corset covers—the hidden architecture of Victorian womanhood, neatly folded in tissue paper. Anna examined each piece carefully, noting the construction, the materials, the small signs of wear that indicated these had been functional garments rather than display pieces. Eleanor had worn these. Her body had pressed against this cotton, been shaped by these seams.

It felt oddly intimate, handling them. More intimate, in some ways, than the letters. These were the things Eleanor had touched every day, had felt against her skin. The private layer beneath the public presentation.

Anna photographed everything, made notes, moved on.

The second box held accessories. Gloves in various lengths, fans, small beaded bags. A collection of mourning jewellery—jet and black enamel—that suggested Eleanor had outlived several family members. A hatpin with an enamel butterfly that had no obvious significance but that Anna found herself studying for a long moment anyway, imagining Eleanor's fingers sliding it through heavy fabric, securing her hat before stepping out into the street.

The third box. The fourth. Day dresses in muted colours—grey, brown, dark blue. Evening wear in silk and velvet. A wedding dress, cream satin now faded to ivory, with a note pinned to the tissue paper in faded pencil: *E.M. Ashworth, married Thomas Blackwood, June 1891.*

Anna paused at that. 1891. The letters she'd found spanned 1887 to 1889. Two years of passion, of Thursdays, of the green silk dress— and then, two years later, a wedding. To a man.

She thought about Eleanor standing at the altar in this cream satin dress, marrying Thomas Blackwood. Had M. made this dress too? Had she stood in her workshop, stitching the bodice, knowing that Eleanor would wear it to bind herself to someone else?

Or had Eleanor gone to a different dressmaker for this one? Had she not been able to bear it—having M.'s hands shape the gar- ment she would wear to her wedding? Had M. even known about the engagement, or had Eleanor simply stopped coming to Thursdays, stopped writing letters, disappeared into the respectable life that had always been expected of her?

The letters didn't say. The letters ended in September 1889, with a note from M. that was shorter than usual, more restrained:

I understand that circumstances change. That what is possible in one season may not be possible in the next. I have asked nothing of you that you did not wish to give, and I will ask nothing now. If you need to step back from our arrangement, I will accept it. I will not make things difficult for you.

But know this: what we have built together does not disappear simply because we cease to meet. You have learned things about yourself that cannot be unlearned. You have become something that you were not before. That belongs to you now—not to me, not to our Thursdays, not to any future husband or any respectable life. To you.

Whatever happens, you will always know what it means to be truly seen.

Yours—

M.

Anna had read that letter a dozen times. It broke her heart every time. The dignity of it. The grief held so carefully in check. M. letting Eleanor go, because that was what Eleanor needed, even though it must have cost her everything.

She set aside the wedding dress and opened the next box.

* * *

Her phone buzzed.

Anna stripped off one glove and checked the screen. Margot.

How's the treasure hunt?

Anna smiled despite herself. She'd told Margot where she'd be today—the textile repository, the Ashworth collection, the search for the dress. Margot had seemed genuinely interested, asking questions about the process, about what Anna hoped to find.

Six boxes down. Eleven to go. No green silk yet. Anna typed back.

The response came quickly: *Keep looking. It's there.*

Such confidence. Anna wondered if Margot was always like this—certain that things would work out, that searches would yield results, that the world would arrange itself according to expectation. It was seductive, that certainty. It made Anna want to believe it too.

She put her phone away and pulled the glove back on.

Box seven. Box eight. More dresses, more accessories, a collection of embroidered handkerchiefs with monograms she didn't recognise. A fur-trimmed cape that smelled faintly of lavender even after all these years. A pair of dancing slippers, pink satin, barely worn—perhaps from Eleanor's youth, before the relationship with M., before any of it.

Anna was beginning to feel the familiar doubt of archival research. The collection was large, the cataloguing was minimal, and there was no guarantee that the dress she was looking for had survived at all. It might have been worn out, given away, lost in some house move or family clearing. It might have been deliberately destroyed—by Eleanor herself, perhaps, trying to erase the evidence of what she'd been, what she'd wanted. People did that sometimes. Burned the letters, threw away the objects, tried to pretend the past had never happened.

Box nine.

Box ten.

Her phone buzzed again.

Dinner Thursday? 7pm, my place. I'll text you the address.

Anna stared at the message. Thursday. The same day of the week that Eleanor and M. had met. Coincidence—Margot didn't know about Thursdays, didn't know the significance—but it sent a small thrill through her anyway.

She thought about what M. might have written, if M. had had a mobile phone instead of pen and paper. Would the messages have been as careful, as composed? Or would the immediacy of texting have stripped away some of the formality, revealed the woman underneath the performance?

Anna tried to imagine M.'s voice saying Margot's words. *Dinner Thursday. My place.* It almost worked. The economy of it, the assumption that Anna would say yes.

But M. would have added something else, Anna thought. An instruction. *Wear the grey dress. Do not speak when you enter. Wait for me to address you.*

Margot hadn't added anything else. Just the invitation, simple and direct. No ritual, no performance. Just: come to my place, I'll cook for you.

Anna typed back: *Thursday works. Looking forward to it.*

Then she added, before she could stop herself: *What should I wear?*

The response came a minute later: *Whatever you're comfortable in. It's just dinner.*

Anna felt something deflate slightly in her chest. Just dinner. She'd known that. What had she expected—that Margot would tell her to wear a specific dress, give her instructions about how to present herself? That wasn't how Margot operated. Margot was modern, practical, direct. Margot asked what you wanted, not what you should be told to want.

It was fine. It was good, even. Healthy. The kind of dynamic that actual relationships were built on—mutual respect, open communication, nobody playing games.

Anna put her phone away and tried not to feel disappointed.

* * *

Box eleven contained household linens—tablecloths, napkins, antimacassars—and Anna was beginning to lose hope. The garments had been in the earlier boxes; perhaps the rest was all domestic goods, the mundane detritus of a long life.

She opened box twelve anyway.

More tissue paper. She parted it carefully, her gloved fingers gentle on the fragile material.

Green silk.

She parted the tissue paper the rest of the way with hands that had gone stupid and slow.

It was folded carefully, the bodice on top, the skirt beneath. The colour had faded—it would have been darker originally, a deep forest green—but it was still recognisably, unmistakably silk. Good quality. Well-made. The kind of dress a respectable gentlewoman would have worn to a dinner party, perhaps. A Michaelmas dinner, with fourteen people in the room.

Anna's hands were trembling as she lifted it from the box.

The dress was heavy. Heavier than it should have been for the fabric weight. She could feel it immediately—something in the construction that added mass where mass shouldn't be.

She carried it to the examination table, spread it out on the clean white cotton. Her conservator's eye took over, assessing: late 1880s construction, bodice boned in the expected places, skirt with moderate bustle support. The seams were neat, professional. High-quality work.

But there was something else.

Anna ran her fingers along the left side seam, feeling through the glove. There. Additional boning, sewn into the lining, extending further than standard construction would require. It would press against the wearer's ribs—not painfully, not obviously, but constantly. A pressure with every breath.

The boning along the left seam will press just slightly with each breath. A reminder.

She kept examining. The bodice seams were taken in slightly tighter than fashion required—not enough to be uncomfortable, but enough to shape the wearer's posture. To hold her straighter than she might naturally stand. And in the skirt, sewn into the hem where no one would see—

Weights. Small metal weights, distributed evenly around the circumference. They would change how the fabric moved, how it fell. They would make the wearer conscious of the skirt's presence with every step, every turn.

Anna stood very still, her hands resting on the fabric.

This was it. This was the dress. M. had made this, had sewn these alterations with her own hands, had created a garment that was also a command. Eleanor had worn it to formal dinners, to social occasions, surrounded by people who had no idea what they were looking at. She had moved through those rooms held by invisible constraints, shaped by M.'s work, carrying their secret pressed against her body.

Anna thought about what that would feel like. To wear something like this. To sit at a table making polite conversation while the boning pressed your ribs and the weights reminded you with every shift of position that someone else had decided how you would move. That even here, even among all these people who couldn't see what was right in front of them, you belonged to someone.

She took out her phone and photographed the dress from every angle. The overall silhouette. The seams. The places where she'd found the alterations. Evidence. Proof. The material reality of something that had lived until now only in words on paper.

Then she stood for a long time, just looking at it.

The green silk lay on the white cotton, faded and fragile and over a hundred years old. It should have felt like history—distant, academic, something to be studied and preserved. Instead it felt like a letter she hadn't known was waiting for her. A message from

Eleanor and M., transmitted through fabric and thread and tiny metal weights.

This is what it looked like. This is what it felt like. This is what we were.

Anna's phone buzzed in her pocket. She checked it, distracted.

Margot: *Any luck?*

Anna looked at the dress. Looked at her phone. Typed:

I found it.

* * *

That evening, Anna spread her transcriptions across her kitchen table and built a timeline.

November 1887: first letter. Eleanor had been visiting M.'s workshop for fittings, but the fittings had become something else. The letters began.

January 1888: the green silk dress. *The modifications we discussed.* M. had made something that would hold Eleanor even when they were apart.

March 1888: Eleanor's letter about the Harrington dinner. *The Harrington dinner last night. Fourteen people in the room and not one of them knew every breath I took was yours.*

June 1888: a gap in the correspondence. No letters for almost two months. Then a brief, pained note from Eleanor: *I am sorry I have been away. Family matters. My mother has been ill. I have not forgotten. I have not stopped thinking of you.*

Autumn 1888: the relationship deepening. More explicit letters, longer passages about what passed between them on Thursdays. Eleanor finding language for things she hadn't been able to name before. M. teaching her—not just techniques, not just positions, but a way of understanding herself.

You ask why I want what I want, Eleanor wrote in October. *I do not know how to answer except to say that when I am with you, I am more myself than I have ever been anywhere else. You have shown me that what I thought was weakness—my desire to yield, to follow, to give over control—is actually a kind of strength. It takes courage to surrender. You have taught me that.*

Winter 1889: something changing. The letters became less frequent. Eleanor wrote about pressure from her family—expectations, obligations, the life she was supposed to be living. M. wrote back with patience and understanding, but also with something that might have been resignation.

I have always known that what we have is borrowed time, M. wrote in February. *I am not of your world, and you cannot stay in mine. That does not make what we have less real. It only makes it finite.*

September 1889: the final letter. M.'s careful goodbye. *Whatever happens, you will always know what it means to be truly seen.*

And then: silence. Two years later, a wedding. Thomas Blackwood. A cream satin dress.

Anna stared at her timeline, her notes spread across the table like a map of someone else's heart. Two years. That's all they'd had. Two years of Thursdays, of letters, of the green silk dress—and then it was over, and Eleanor had married a man and lived another fifty-four years and never, as far as Anna could tell, mentioned M. again.

But she'd kept the letters. Hidden them in a book, where no one would find them. And she'd kept the dress—hadn't worn it out, hadn't given it away, hadn't destroyed it. She'd kept it, all through her marriage, all through her long life, until someone donated it to a university repository where it had sat for seventeen years waiting for Anna to find it.

That meant something. It had to mean something.

Anna thought about Margot. About Thursday. About the dinner invitation that had come with no instructions, no ritual, just: come over, I'll cook.

She thought about M.'s letters, the careful structure of them. The way M. had built a framework for Eleanor's surrender, given her something to lean against. Permission to want what she wanted. A shape for her need.

Margot wasn't like that. Margot was direct, modern, practical. Margot asked what you wanted instead of telling you what to want.

She told herself this was how relationships worked. That asking was better than assuming. That the openness Margot offered was the thing she should want.

Anna gathered up her papers and went to bed.

She didn't sleep well.

The next morning, she woke to a text from Margot: *Tell me about the dress. I want to hear everything.*

Anna lay in bed, phone in hand, and typed a response. Then deleted it. Typed again. Deleted again.

How could she explain what she'd found? The alterations, the weights, the way M. had built obedience into the very structure of the garment? It would sound strange, she thought. Obsessive. Like she was reading too much into old fabric, finding meaning where there was only sewing.

But Margot had asked. Margot had said she wanted to know.

Anna typed: *It's hard to explain over text. Can I tell you Thursday?*

The response came quickly: *I'll hold you to that. See you at 7.*

I'll hold you to that.

Anna read the words three times. Such an ordinary phrase. People said it all the time—I'll hold you to that, meaning: don't forget, I'm counting on you, I expect you to follow through.

But Anna heard it differently. She heard M.'s voice underneath, the careful composure of the letters. She heard a promise hidden in plain sight, the way M. had hidden alterations in the seams of a green silk dress.

I'll hold you.

Anna got up and went to work, and tried not to count the hours until Thursday.

CHAPTER 7

Margot's flat was on the second floor of a Victorian conversion in Jericho, up a narrow staircase that smelled faintly of old wood and someone else's cooking. Anna climbed it with her heart beating too fast, a bottle of wine in her hand that she'd spent twenty minutes choosing and still wasn't sure about.

The door was already open when she reached the landing. Margot stood in the doorway, backlit by warm light, wearing a soft grey shirt with the sleeves rolled up and dark trousers that looked like they'd been chosen for comfort rather than impression.

"You found it," she said, smiling.

"Your directions were good."

"I'm very precise." Margot stepped back, gesturing Anna inside. "Professional habit. Come in—I'm just finishing up."

The flat was smaller than Anna had expected, and warmer. The main room combined kitchen and living space, separated by a wooden counter that served as both workspace and dining table. Bookshelves lined one wall, stuffed with paperbacks in several languages. A worn leather sofa faced a window that looked out over the street. Everything felt lived-in, comfortable, unapologetically itself.

The kitchen end of the room was where the energy was. Margot moved back to the stove, where something was simmering in a heavy copper pan. The counter was organised chaos—chopping boards, herb stems, a bowl of something dark and glossy that might have been a reduction. Anna could smell garlic and wine and something deeper underneath, rich and meaty.

"Sit," Margot said, nodding toward a stool at the counter. "Talk to me while I finish. And open that wine—there's a corkscrew in the drawer by the fridge."

Anna felt the instruction land in her spine. Such a small thing —*open that wine*—but the casual authority of it, the assumption that Anna would comply, sent a pulse of heat through her chest. She found the corkscrew, opened the bottle, poured two glasses without being told to. When she set one beside Margot's cutting board, Margot glanced at her with a small smile that might have meant anything.

"Thank you."

Anna sat on the stool and watched her cook.

It was like watching her in the canteen kitchen, but more intimate. No staff, no service pressure, no need to maintain the professional facade. Margot moved with the same efficiency, the same certainty, but there was something looser about it here. She tasted from a spoon and made a face—not quite right—added a pinch of something, tasted again. Nodded to herself. Adjusted the heat under the pan with a quick, decisive turn of the dial.

"You're staring," she said, without looking up.

"I like watching you cook."

"I know." Now she did look up, her eyes warm with amusement. "You've been watching me cook for weeks. I'm starting to think it's your kink."

The word landed like a small shock. Anna felt her face heat. "I—"

"Relax." Margot's voice was gentle. "I'm teasing. Mostly." She turned back to the stove, stirring something. "Tell me about the dress. You said you'd explain in person."

Anna took a breath. She'd been thinking about this all week—how to explain what she'd found, how to make Margot understand why it mattered. She'd rehearsed versions in her head, discarded them, started over.

"It's a green silk evening dress," she began. "Late 1880s. Good quality, well-made. The kind of thing a respectable woman would wear to a dinner party." She paused. "But there are alterations. Hidden ones. Extra boning along one side seam, so it presses against the ribs with every breath. The bodice taken in tighter than necessary, so the wearer has to stand straighter. And weights sewn into the hem—small metal weights, distributed evenly, so the skirt moves differently. So you're aware of it with every step."

Margot had stopped stirring. She was looking at Anna now, her expression thoughtful.

"The dressmaker made it that way," Anna continued. "M. She made a dress that would—hold Eleanor. Remind her. Even when they were apart, even in a room full of people who had no idea, Eleanor would feel M.'s work against her body. The letters talk about it. Eleanor wore it to a dinner with fourteen people and nobody knew except the two of them."

"A secret," Margot said slowly. "In plain sight."

"Yes." Anna's voice had gone quiet. "That's what I keep thinking about. The way you could—carry something like that with you. Into the rest of your life. The way the structure of it would shape you, even when you were alone."

Margot was silent for a moment. Then she turned back to the stove, gave the pan one final stir, and switched off the heat.

"That's beautiful," she said. "And a little bit heartbreaking."

"Why heartbreaking?"

"Because it ended." Margot began plating the food—some kind of braised meat with vegetables, it smelled incredible—her movements precise and unhurried. "You said the letters only cover two years. And then Eleanor married someone else. So all that—the dress, the Thursdays, the whole careful structure they built—it didn't last. It couldn't."

Anna hadn't expected that response. She'd been so focused on the romance of it—the hidden intimacy, the secret shared across a crowded room—that she'd almost forgotten the ending. The cream satin wedding dress. The fifty-four years of marriage to Thomas Blackwood.

"But she kept the dress," Anna said. "And the letters. Her whole life, she kept them."

"That's something." Margot set a plate in front of Anna, then came around the counter with her own and sat on the stool beside her. Close, but not quite touching. "It's not nothing, keeping the evidence. Even if you can't live the life."

They ate. The food was, predictably, excellent—the meat falling apart, the sauce rich with wine and herbs, the vegetables perfectly cooked. Anna made appreciative noises and meant them.

"This is incredible," she said. "Where did you learn to cook like this?"

"Practice. Stubbornness. A lot of burnt pans in my twenties." Margot shrugged. "I never went to culinary school or anything. Just figured it out as I went. Found people who knew more than me and paid attention."

"That's how I learned conservation," Anna said. "Apprentice-ship, mostly. Watching people who'd been doing it for decades. Learning to see what they saw."

"Learning to see." Margot tilted her head. "I like that. That's what it is, isn't it? Most skills. Learning to notice what other people miss."

Their eyes met. Anna felt something shift in the air between them—a charge, a possibility.

"You see a lot," she said quietly. "Don't you?"

"I try to." Margot's voice had dropped too, gone soft and warm. "I've been watching you too, you know. Not just in the canteen. Tonight. The way you responded when I told you to open the wine. The way you're sitting right now, like you're waiting for instructions."

She hadn't realised—but now that Margot said it, she could feel it. The slight tension in her posture. The way she'd oriented toward Margot without meaning to.

"I'm not—" she started, then stopped. She didn't know how to finish that sentence.

"You don't have to be anything," Margot said. "You don't have to perform. I just—I notice. That's all."

She reached out and touched Anna's hand where it rested on the counter. Just her fingertips, light and warm.

"Come sit with me," she said. "On the couch. Bring your wine."

* * *

The couch was soft, worn in a way that suggested years of use. Anna sank into it, her wine glass cradled in both hands, acutely aware of Margot settling beside her. Close enough that their knees almost touched.

"Can I ask you something?" Margot said.

"Yes."

"When you read those letters—the first time, I mean, before you knew what they were—what did you feel?"

Anna considered the question. She could give an easy answer—fascination, curiosity, academic interest. But Margot had asked what she *felt*, and she'd promised herself she would try to be honest.

"Recognition," she said finally. "Like I was reading something I already knew but didn't have words for. The way Eleanor wrote about wanting to surrender—wanting to be told what to do, wanting to give over control—it wasn't unfamiliar. It was just... the first time I'd seen it written down. The first time I understood it was a real thing, not just something broken in me."

Margot set her wine glass on the side table. She turned toward Anna, one knee drawing up onto the couch, her full attention focused.

"You thought you were broken?"

"Didn't you?" Anna heard the rawness in her own voice. "Before you figured it out? Before you had language for it? I spent years thinking there was something wrong with me. That I couldn't connect properly, couldn't want the right things, couldn't—" She broke off, shaking her head.

"Yes," Margot said quietly. "I remember that. Feeling like I was playing a role in relationships, going through motions that didn't mean anything. It took me a long time to understand that the problem wasn't me—it was that I was trying to fit myself into scripts that didn't work for me."

"How did you figure it out?"

"I met someone." A small smile crossed Margot's face, complicated and fond. "A woman who was very patient with me. Who asked questions I didn't know how to answer and then gave me space to figure them out. She's the one who taught me that there are different ways to be in a relationship. That what I wanted wasn't wrong—it just needed the right context."

"What happened with her?"

"We were together for three years. Then life happened—she got a job in Edinburgh, I wasn't ready to leave Oxford. We're still friends." Margot shrugged. "It wasn't tragic. We just wanted different things, eventually."

Anna absorbed this. Margot had history, experience, a past that had shaped her into the person she was now. Of course she did. But it made Anna feel young somehow, untested. Like she was just starting a journey Margot had already been on.

"I don't really know what I want," she admitted. "I know what the letters made me feel. I know what I imagine, when I'm alone. But actually being with someone—actually doing any of it—I don't know."

"That's okay." Margot's hand found hers, lacing their fingers together. "You don't have to know. Not yet. That's what figuring it out looks like."

Anna looked at their joined hands. Margot's fingers were strong, certain. Kitchen hands.

"Can I—" She stopped, started again. "I want to kiss you. Is that—"

"Yes," Margot said, and closed the distance between them.

The kiss was soft at first. Tentative. Margot's lips were warm, tasting faintly of wine, and she let Anna set the pace—let her lean in, explore, figure out what she was doing. It was gentle in a way that made Anna's chest ache.

Then something shifted.

Margot's hand came up to cup the back of Anna's neck, and suddenly the kiss wasn't tentative anymore. It was deep, thorough, the kind of kiss that demanded a response. Anna heard herself make a small sound—surprise, pleasure, both—and Margot swallowed it, pulling her closer.

This. *This* was what she'd been waiting for. Margot's hand on her neck, firm and sure. Margot's mouth taking control of the kiss, not asking, not waiting, just *taking*. Anna felt herself go liquid, her body softening, yielding.

Margot pulled back slightly, breathing hard.

"Okay?" she asked.

"Yes." Anna's voice came out breathless. "Very okay."

Margot smiled, slow and pleased, and kissed her again.

Time went strange. Anna lost track of it—lost track of everything except Margot's mouth, Margot's hands, the heat building between them. At some point she ended up half in Margot's lap, one of Margot's hands tangled in her hair, the other sliding under the hem of her shirt to rest on the bare skin of her waist. The touch was electric. Anna gasped against Margot's lips and felt Margot smile.

"Sensitive," Margot murmured. "Good to know."

She traced patterns on Anna's skin—circles, lines, nothing coherent—and Anna shivered with each stroke. It felt so good. Margot's confidence, her sureness, the way she touched Anna like she had every right to. Like she was learning Anna's body through her fingertips.

But somewhere underneath the pleasure, a small voice whispered: *this isn't quite right.*

Anna tried to ignore it. She was here, in Margot's lap, being kissed within an inch of her life. This was good. This was what she wanted.

Wasn't it?

Margot's hand slid higher, brushing the underwire of Anna's bra, and Anna's breath stuttered.

"Still okay?" Margot asked, pulling back to check her face.

"Yes." Anna heard the slight hesitation in her own voice and hated it. "Yes, I'm—it's good."

Margot studied her for a moment. Then she withdrew her hand, slowly, and settled it on Anna's hip instead.

"We don't have to rush," she said. "There's no deadline here."

Anna felt a confusing mix of relief and disappointment. She wanted—what did she want? She wanted Margot to keep touching her. She also wanted something else, something she couldn't quite name. A shape that Margot wasn't fitting into.

Tell me what to do, she thought. *Give me instructions. Make me hold still.*

But she didn't say it. She didn't know how to say it without sounding like she was asking Margot to be someone she wasn't.

"I'm enjoying this," she said instead. "I just—it's been a while. For me."

"How long?"

Anna thought about it. "Two years? Almost three. Since my last girlfriend."

"Then we'll take it slow." Margot's thumb traced circles on Anna's hip, soothing. "I'm not going anywhere."

She pulled Anna back down for another kiss, softer this time. Sweeter. Anna let herself sink into it, tried to quiet the voice in her head that kept comparing this to something it wasn't.

Margot was lovely. Margot was attentive and confident and clearly knew what she was doing. The way she kissed, the way her hands moved—there was authority in it, just not the kind Anna had been imagining. Margot didn't give orders. She asked questions. She checked in. She made sure Anna was comfortable at every step.

The right way to do things. She knew that.

Anna told herself that, and kissed Margot back, and tried not to notice the gap between what was happening and what she'd built in her head.

* * *

They stayed on the couch for a long time, kissing, talking, kissing again. The wine glasses sat forgotten on the side table. The light outside the window shifted from evening to true dark.

At some point Margot said, "It's getting late. You should probably head home."

Anna didn't want to go. But she also knew, somewhere beneath the pleasant haze of wine and desire, that if she stayed longer things would progress. And she wasn't ready. Not yet. Not while she was still sorting out what she wanted from what she'd imagined.

"Probably," she agreed.

Margot walked her to the door. In the narrow hallway, with the dim light from the stairwell filtering up, she looked softer than she did in her kitchen. Less certain. Almost nervous.

"I had a really good time tonight," she said.

"Me too." Anna meant it. Whatever her complicated feelings, the evening had been good. Margot had been good.

"Can I see you again? Soon?"

"Yes." No hesitation on that one. "I'd like that."

Margot smiled, and something in her face eased. She'd been worried, Anna realised. Unsure if the evening had gone well. It was oddly reassuring—a reminder that Margot was human too, not just the confident figure Anna had built her into.

"Good." Margot stepped closer and kissed her one more time —quick, warm, a promise. "Text me when you get home safe."

"I will."

Anna walked down the stairs and out into the cold November night. Her lips were swollen from kissing. Her body still hummed with want. She thought about Margot's hands, Margot's mouth, the way Margot had asked *still okay?* every time she did something new.

She thought about M., who hadn't asked. Who had told Eleanor to stand still and expected her to obey.

Different dynamics. Different people. Different eras, different expectations, different everything. It wasn't fair to compare Margot to a woman who had died a century ago, whose voice Anna knew only through carefully composed letters. The real M. had probably asked questions too. Had probably checked in, negotiated, adjusted. The letters were a highlight reel, not the whole relationship.

She walked home through the quiet streets with swollen lips and the taste of wine still in her mouth. She liked Margot. She wanted to see Margot again. The kissing had been the best kissing of her life, which was a fact, not a performance.

But there had been something missing. Some quality she'd been reaching for that hadn't quite materialised.

It's early, she told herself. These things take time. You can't expect someone to know exactly what you need when you haven't told them. When you barely know yourself.

She texted Margot from her doorstep: *Home safe. Thank you for dinner. And everything else.*

The response came a minute later: *Glad you made it. Sleep well. I'm already thinking about next time.*

Anna smiled at her phone in the dark. Next time. There would be a next time.

But at two in the morning she woke up in her cold flat and reached for her laptop and opened the transcription file and read M.'s letters until the sky turned grey.

That probably meant something. She wasn't ready to think about what.

CHAPTER 8

The conservation workroom was quiet on Friday afternoons. Marcus had left early—something about a dentist appointment—and Dr. Fitzwilliam was in London for a conference. Anna had the space to herself, the familiar hum of the climate control system, the grey November light falling through the high windows.

She was supposed to be working on the Ashworth household accounts. Condition assessment, provenance notes, the steady accumulation of documentation that was her job. But her hands kept drifting to the photographs on her laptop—the green silk dress, spread out on the examination table in the textile repository. The hidden boning. The weighted hem. The evidence of a relationship built into fabric.

She'd requested permission to bring the dress to her own conservation lab for closer examination. The paperwork was still processing. In the meantime, she had the photographs, and she had the letters, and she had far too much time alone with both.

Her phone buzzed. Margot.

Thinking about Thursday. Can't stop, actually.

Anna smiled despite herself. Thursday had been—good. Genuinely good. Margot's flat, the dinner, the kissing that had gone on for hours. She should be thinking about that. Should be replaying those moments, anticipating the next time.

Instead, she was staring at a photograph of a dress that a dead woman had worn to dinner parties a hundred and thirty years ago.

Thinking about you too, she typed back. It was true. She was thinking about Margot. Just not only about Margot.

She set the phone aside and opened her transcription file.

The letters didn't describe every occasion Eleanor had worn the dress. There was the Michaelmas dinner—*fourteen people in the room and only you knew*—but that was a single reference, a few lines. Anna wanted more. She wanted to see it: the room, the guests, the dress doing its secret work while Eleanor made polite conversation.

She found herself imagining it. Not reading, not researching—just letting the scene build in her mind. The dining room in Eleanor's family home. Candlelight. The heavy fabric of the dress pressing against Eleanor's ribs with each breath.

What if M. had been there?

The letters never mentioned such an evening. But it wasn't impossible. Victorian hostesses sometimes invited local tradespeople to charitable dinners, especially around Christmas. A gesture of noblesse oblige. The dressmaker, the milliner, the better sort of merchant—elevated for an evening, seated at the same table as the family they served.

Anna closed her eyes. Let the scene take shape.

* * *

Eleanor's mother called it the Tradesmen's Supper, though never where the guests could hear. A December tradition, instituted by Eleanor's grandmother and maintained out of obligation rather than enthusiasm. The better merchants and craftspeople of the town, invited to dine with the Ashworth family once a year. A reminder that the gentry appreciated those who served them. A performance of Christian charity.

Eleanor had endured these evenings since childhood. The awkward conversation, the guests who didn't know which fork to use, her mother's tight smile as she navigated the social complexities of entertaining people she would normally address through the servants' entrance. It was tedious, uncomfortable, and mercifully brief.

This year was different.

This year, M. would be there.

Eleanor had seen the guest list that morning, had watched her mother's finger move down the names—the greengrocer, the clockmaker, the woman who ran the stationer's shop—and stop at *Miss M. Thorne, Dressmaker*. Her mother had frowned slightly. "I suppose we must include her. She does good work, and Mrs. Ashworth-Clarke recommended her most highly."

Eleanor had said nothing. Had kept her face perfectly composed, her hands folded in her lap. But her heart had begun to pound, and it hadn't stopped since.

Now she stood in her bedroom, looking at herself in the mirror, wearing the green silk dress.

M. had delivered it three weeks ago. Had fitted it herself, her hands moving along Eleanor's seams with professional efficiency while Eleanor stood frozen, barely breathing. The alterations were invisible to anyone who didn't know to look for them. But Eleanor knew. She felt the extra boning press against her left side, felt the slight constriction of the too-tight bodice, felt the unfamiliar weight of the hem pulling at her with every step.

She looked respectable. Modest. A gentlewoman dressed appropriately for a charitable dinner. No one would see anything amiss.

M. would see everything.

Eleanor pressed her hand flat against her ribs, where the boning pressed back. A reminder. A presence. Even when they were apart, M. had said, this would hold her. And it did. It had been holding her for weeks now—through morning calls and afternoon tea and endless family dinners—and tonight M. would be in the room to witness it.

Her maid appeared in the doorway. "They're asking for you downstairs, miss. The guests are arriving."

Eleanor took one last look at herself in the mirror. The woman who looked back was composed, appropriate, invisible.

Inside the dress, she was someone else entirely.

* * *

The drawing room was warm with firelight and bodies. Eleanor's father stood by the hearth, making conversation with the clockmaker about the weather. Her mother circulated with practiced grace, offering sherry and empty pleasantries. The guests clustered in awkward groups—merchants who knew each other from the high street but had never seen each other in evening dress, uncertain how to behave in a house so much grander than their own.

Eleanor stood near the window, a glass of sherry untouched in her hand, and watched the door.

She saw M. the moment she entered.

The dressmaker wore deep grey—practical, understated, nothing that would draw attention. Her dark hair was pinned up simply, without ornament. She carried herself with the careful neutrality of someone who understood exactly where she stood in the room's hierarchy and had no intention of disrupting it.

To anyone watching, she was simply another tradeswoman, grateful for the invitation, conscious of the honour.

Eleanor knew better.

M.'s eyes swept the room—quick, assessing—and found Eleanor by the window. The contact lasted less than a second. An acknowledgment, nothing more. Then M. turned to accept a glass of sherry from a passing servant, and Eleanor was left with her heart pounding and the boning pressing against her ribs and a flush rising in her cheeks that she desperately hoped could be attributed to the fire.

Dinner was announced. The guests moved toward the dining room in rough order of precedence—Eleanor's parents first, then the family friends who had been invited to leaven the social awkwardness, then the tradespeople in a shuffling mass. Eleanor hung back, ostensibly to ensure everyone found their seats.

M. passed within arm's reach. She didn't look at Eleanor. Didn't acknowledge her at all. But as she passed, her voice came low and private, pitched for Eleanor's ears alone:

"Straighten your shoulders."

Three words. That was all. And then M. was gone, following the other guests into the dining room, and Eleanor was left standing in the doorway with her spine snapping straight and heat flooding her entire body.

She straightened her shoulders. She had been told to.

————

The seating arrangement, by some accident of her mother's planning, placed M. directly across the table from Eleanor. Not next to her—that would have been too intimate, too noticeable. But in her line of sight for the entire meal.

Eleanor didn't know if M. had arranged this somehow, or if fate had simply conspired in their favour. It didn't matter. What mattered was that for the next two hours, every time she raised her eyes from her plate, she would see M. watching her.

The first course was soup. Eleanor lifted her spoon with hands that trembled only slightly. She was aware of M.'s gaze on her—not constant, not obvious, but present. Checking. Assessing.

She kept her shoulders straight.

"Miss Ashworth," the clockmaker said from her left, "I understand you've been studying watercolours. My daughter has taken an interest as well. Perhaps you might recommend a tutor?"

Eleanor turned to answer him, grateful for the distraction. She spoke about watercolours, about tutors, about the improving nature of artistic pursuits. Normal conversation. The kind of thing she'd done a thousand times.

But underneath her words, underneath the social performance, she was exquisitely aware of the dress. The boning pressing with each breath. The bodice holding her straighter than she would naturally stand. The weights in the hem, reminding her of their presence every time she shifted in her chair.

M. had built this. Had sewn these constraints into the fabric with her own hands. And now she sat across the table, eating soup with perfect composure, and watched Eleanor be held.

Eleanor risked a glance across the table. M.'s expression was neutral, polite—the face of a tradeswoman honoured to be included, grateful for the opportunity. But her eyes, when they met Eleanor's, held something else entirely.

I see you, those eyes said.

Eleanor kept her eyes on her plate and counted the tines of her fish fork.

The fish course came and went. The meat. Eleanor made conversation with the guests on either side of her, discussed the weather and the state of the roads and the upcoming Christmas celebrations. She was a perfect hostess. She was a perfect daughter. No one could have faulted her behaviour.

But every few minutes, her eyes drifted across the table. And every time, M. was already watching.

It was unbearable. It was exquisite. Eleanor felt herself dissolving into the tension of it—the ache of wanting to be acknowledged, the torture of being seen but not touched, the impossible position of sitting at her family's dinner table while the woman across from her held her captive with nothing but a gaze and a dress that wouldn't let her forget.

She reached for her water glass. Her hand was shaking. She saw M. notice, saw the slight curve of M.'s lips that might have been satisfaction.

"Are you quite well, dear?" her mother asked from the head of the table. "You look flushed."

"The fire," Eleanor said. "It's rather warm in here."

"Shall I have someone open a window?"

"No—no, I'm fine. Thank you."

She didn't dare look at M. She could feel M.'s amusement from across the table anyway.

* * *

After dinner, the guests retired to the drawing room for coffee and conversation. The women clustered by the fire; the men stood near the windows with their port. Eleanor was supposed to circulate, to make the guests feel welcome, to perform the duties of a daughter of the house.

Instead, she found herself standing near the doorway, watching M. across the room.

The dressmaker was speaking with the milliner—professional courtesy, perhaps, or simply the gravitational pull of tradespeople toward each other in an unfamiliar social setting. She held her coffee cup with easy grace, her posture relaxed, her expression pleasant and unremarkable.

No one looking at her would see anything unusual. A woman in her thirties, respectable, skilled at her trade. Perhaps unmarried, perhaps widowed—the grey dress gave no hints. Nothing about her suggested that she spent Thursday afternoons teaching a gentleman's daughter how to kneel. How to wait. How to hold still until given permission to move.

Eleanor watched her, and wanted, and could do nothing about any of it.

M. looked up. Caught Eleanor's gaze. Held it for one long, charged moment.

Then she set down her coffee cup and excused herself from the milliner with a polite word. She crossed the room, not toward Eleanor but toward the door—as if she were simply going to use the retiring room, or to get some air. Nothing noteworthy.

As she passed Eleanor, she murmured: "The library. Two minutes."

And then she was gone, slipping through the door and into the hallway beyond, and Eleanor was left standing with her heart in her throat and a decision to make.

She should stay. She should continue circulating, playing hostess, being the daughter her parents expected. The risk was enormous—someone might notice, might follow, might see—

She counted to one hundred and twenty. Then she set down her own coffee cup, murmured something to the woman beside her about checking on the servants, and walked out of the drawing room.

* * *

The library was dark except for the fire, banked low in the grate. M. stood by the window, her silhouette sharp against the faint glow of the street lamps outside. She didn't turn when Eleanor entered. Didn't acknowledge her at all.

Eleanor closed the door behind her. The click of the latch sounded impossibly loud in the silence.

"Come here."

Two words. Eleanor's feet carried her across the carpet before her mind had finished processing the command. She stopped an arm's length from M., who still hadn't turned around. Who was making her wait.

"You wore it," M. said quietly. "I wasn't sure you would."

"I—" Eleanor's voice caught. "You asked me to."

"I suggested it. There's a difference." Now M. did turn, and her face in the firelight was unreadable. "You could have worn something else. No one would have known."

"I would have known."

M. smiled. It was a small thing, barely visible, but Eleanor felt it like a reward.

"How does it feel?" M. asked. "Sitting across from me at dinner, wearing my work against your skin?"

Eleanor swallowed. "Unbearable. I couldn't—every time I looked at you—"

"I know." M. stepped closer. Close enough that Eleanor could smell her—something clean and faintly floral, underneath the practical scent of wool and starch. "I watched you. Every moment. The way you sat, the way you breathed. You were perfect."

The word went through Eleanor like a current. *Perfect.* She had been perfect. M. had seen, and approved.

"We don't have long," M. said. "Someone will notice you're gone. But I wanted—" She paused, seeming to choose her words. "I wanted you to know that I saw. Everything you did tonight, everything you endured—I saw it. It mattered."

"It mattered to me too," Eleanor whispered.

M. raised her hand and laid it flat against Eleanor's ribs, exactly where the hidden boning pressed. The touch was light, but Eleanor felt it through every layer of fabric, every carefully constructed seam. M.'s hand, on her body, in her family's library, while a room full of guests waited just down the hall.

"Here," M. said softly. "I've been here all evening. Holding you. Even when I couldn't touch you."

Eleanor made a sound—half gasp, half sob. She wanted to collapse into M., wanted to be held properly, wanted Thursday to be now instead of four days away. But they had minutes at most, stolen seconds in a darkened room, and M. was already stepping back.

"Go back," M. said. "Before someone notices."

"I don't want to."

"I know." M.'s voice was gentle but firm. "But you will. Because I'm telling you to."

Eleanor stood very still. The command hung in the air between them—quiet, absolute.

"Yes," she said. It came out barely a whisper.

M. smiled again, and this time the smile reached her eyes. "Good girl. Thursday. Don't be late."

She turned and left by the library's other door, the one that led to the servants' corridor. Eleanor stood alone in the firelight, her hand pressed to her ribs where M.'s hand had been, and counted to one hundred before she made herself walk back to the drawing room.

No one had noticed she'd gone.

* * *

Anna opened her eyes.

The workroom was silent. The grey afternoon light had faded into early evening, and she was alone at her bench, her laptop screen gone dark, the Ashworth household accounts forgotten beside her.

She didn't know how long she'd been sitting there. Didn't know when the daydream had started, or when it had shifted from idle wondering into something so vivid she could almost smell the firelight and candle wax. The Ashworth household accounts were still open beside her, untouched.

But it had felt so real. Eleanor's dress pressing against her ribs. M.'s voice in the darkness. *Good girl. Thursday. Don't be late.*

Anna's body was still responding as if it had actually happened. Her breath was shallow, her skin warm. She pressed her hand to her side, half expecting to feel boning beneath her jumper.

This was getting out of hand.

Her phone buzzed. She checked it, grateful for the interruption.

Margot: *Dinner again soon? I miss your face.*

Anna stared at the message. A real woman, asking to see her. A woman who had kissed her, touched her, looked at her with genuine interest. A woman who was here, now, alive, not a ghost constructed from old paper and Anna's overactive imagination.

She typed back: *Yes. When are you free?*

The response came immediately: *Tomorrow night? Come over. I'll make something simple.*

Anna hesitated. Tomorrow was Saturday. She had no plans. There was no reason to say no.

Except that part of her wanted to stay home and read the letters again. Wanted to sink back into the fantasy she'd just built, elaborate on it, live there instead of in the messier, less scripted world where real women sent casual text messages and asked what she wanted instead of telling her.

That's not healthy, she told herself. *That's not what you actually want. You want a real relationship. You want Margot.*

She typed: *Tomorrow works. What time?*

Seven? And Anna— A pause, the three dots indicating Margot was still typing. Then: *I'm really looking forward to seeing you.*

Anna closed her eyes. *Real*, she reminded herself. *Margot is real. Focus on what's real.*

Me too, she typed back.

She meant it. She did.

She just wished she meant it more than she meant everything else.

CHAPTER 9

Saturday evening. Margot's flat again—the same warm light, the same worn sofa, the same garlic-and-wine smell drifting from the kitchen.

But something was different tonight. Anna could feel it in the air—a charge, an anticipation. The way Margot looked at her when she opened the door, her gaze lingering a beat too long. The way their hands kept finding each other as they moved around the kitchen, brushing past, not quite accidental.

Dinner was simple—pasta with a sauce Margot threw together while Anna sat at the counter and watched. They drank wine and talked about nothing important: a difficult customer at the canteen, a water-damaged manuscript Anna was working on, the forecast for the coming week. Easy conversation. The comfortable rhythm of two people who were beginning to know each other.

But underneath the words, something else was building.

They moved to the sofa after dinner. Anna tucked herself into the corner, wine glass in hand, and Margot settled beside her—closer than last time. Their thighs touched through their clothes.

"I've been thinking about you," Margot said. "All week."

"I've been thinking about you too."

"Have you?" Margot's hand came to rest on Anna's knee. Light, warm, not moving. "What have you been thinking?"

Anna's breath caught. This was the moment where she could tell the truth—*I've been thinking about Victorian letters and hidden boning and a dressmaker who knew how to give commands*—or she could say something simpler. Something that wouldn't require explanation.

"About this," she said. "About being here with you."

Margot smiled. Her hand slid higher, fingers tracing slow circles on Anna's thigh. "This is good. Being here with you."

"Yes."

"I want to make it better." Margot's voice dropped, went soft and warm. "Can I?"

Anna nodded. She didn't trust her voice.

Margot leaned in and kissed her, and this time there was no hesitation. Her mouth was confident, thorough, demanding a response. Anna gave it—opened to her, let herself be kissed, let Margot's hand slide higher still until it rested at the crease of her hip.

"Bedroom," Margot murmured against her lips. It wasn't quite a question.

Something in Anna's chest tightened—yes, this, the direction she'd been waiting for—

"Yes," she said. "Yes."

* * *

Margot's bedroom was small and neat—a large bed with a dark blue duvet, curtains drawn, a single lamp casting warm light. Margot guided Anna to the edge of the bed and stood in front of her.

"I want to undress you."

Anna nodded, and Margot's hands went to her buttons. She worked them slowly, knuckles brushing skin with each one. The blouse fell open. Margot pushed it off her shoulders and looked at her —the plain cotton bra, the pale skin, the slight softness at her waist.

"Lie back. Let me look at you."

Anna lay back. The duvet was cool beneath her shoulders. She watched Margot pull her own shirt off revealing a sports bra underneath, the practical build of someone who'd spent years lifting and carrying. Margot climbed onto the bed and straddled her thighs and looked down at her with an expression that was warm and focused and real.

"Tell me what you like," she said.

Anna's mind went blank. She'd spent years having sex she didn't want and then years not having sex at all and then weeks reading about a kind of sex she'd never had, and none of that equipped her to answer the question.

"I don't... I'm not sure," she said. "It's been a while."

"That's fine." Margot's thumbs traced slow circles on her ribs. "We'll figure it out together. Tell me if something doesn't work."

She leaned down and kissed Anna's collarbone, her shoulder, the curve of her breast. Unclipped her bra with practised ease. Her mouth found Anna's nipple and Anna gasped, and when Margot used her teeth—just lightly—Anna's hips jerked.

"Noted," Margot murmured, and there was satisfaction in it.

She worked her way down. Kissing Anna's ribs, her stomach, the soft skin below her navel. Unbuttoned her jeans and tugged them off, then her underwear—slow and deliberate—and settled between Anna's legs.

"Relax," she said. "I've got you."

Her mouth found Anna, and for a while thought did scatter. Margot was skilled and unhurried and she was paying attention—staying with the rhythms that worked, adjusting when Anna's body told her to. At one point Anna's hips rose off the bed and Margot pressed a hand flat against her stomach to hold her down, and something lit up in Anna's chest—*yes, that, hold me still*—and then the hand moved away to grip her thigh instead and the moment collapsed back into what it was. Practical, not intentional. Better access, not a command.

She tried to stay in her body. Margot's mouth on her. The pleasure building. She was close—she could feel it—

"What do you need?" Margot lifted her head. "Tell me what'll get you there."

Anna wanted to say *don't ask me, just decide*, and couldn't, and said "Keep doing what you were doing" instead.

She added her fingers this time—two, sliding inside, curling to find the spot that made Anna's whole body jolt. Her mouth and hand worked together, building a rhythm that was impossible to resist. Anna felt herself climbing toward the edge, her hands fisting in the duvet, her breath coming in ragged gasps—

"That's it," Margot murmured against her. "Let go. I want to feel you come."

I want to feel you come. It wasn't a command. It was a request. A desire. Margot wanted something, and Anna could give it to her—

She came. The orgasm rolled through her in long, shuddering waves, and she cried out—Margot's name, or something wordless, she couldn't tell—and Margot stayed with her through all of it, gentling her touches as the sensation peaked and faded, easing her back down.

"God," Anna breathed. Her whole body was trembling. "That was—"

"Good?" Margot crawled up beside her, propped on one elbow, looking pleased with herself.

"Very good."

"Good." Margot kissed her—soft, unhurried—and Anna could taste herself on Margot's lips. It should have been strange. It wasn't. It was intimate in a way that made her chest ache.

"Your turn," Anna said, when the kiss ended. "Tell me what you want."

Margot's smile shifted into something hungrier. "I want your hands on me. Can you do that?"

"Yes."

Anna rolled toward her, pushed her onto her back. Margot went willingly, spreading beneath her, and for a moment Anna felt something like power—she was on top now, she was in control—

But Margot's hand came up to cup the back of her neck, guiding her down for another kiss, and the dynamic shifted back. Even from below, even with Anna technically on top, Margot was leading. Setting the pace. Deciding.

That was fine. That was good. Anna didn't want to be in charge anyway.

She worked her way down Margot's body—less gracefully than Margot had, more uncertain—and Margot helped her, shifting to remove her bra, lifting her hips so Anna could pull off her underwear. Naked, she was stunning: strong and curved and utterly unselfconscious.

"Here," Margot said, taking Anna's hand and guiding it between her legs. "Like this."

She was wet, slick and hot, and Anna's fingers slid against her easily. Margot made a sound—low, pleased—and her hips rocked up into the touch.

"That's good. A little higher—yes, there—"

She was directing. Telling Anna what to do, where to touch, how fast to move. It was practical, communicative, exactly what sex was supposed to be—two people figuring out what worked, talking to each other, building something together.

It wasn't what Anna wanted.

She wanted to be told, not taught. She wanted commands, not suggestions. She wanted Margot to say *do this* and expect obedience, not *try this* and offer guidance.

But that wasn't fair. That wasn't Margot's fault. Anna had never told her what she wanted—had never articulated it, never asked. How was Margot supposed to know?

Anna pushed the thoughts away and focused on Margot's body. The sounds she made, the way her hips moved, the increasing urgency of her breath. She was getting close—Anna could feel it in the way her muscles tensed, the way her hand gripped Anna's shoulder.

"Faster," Margot gasped. "Right there—don't stop—"

Anna didn't stop. She kept her rhythm steady, her focus on Margot's face, watching the pleasure build. And when Margot came —head thrown back, a sharp cry escaping her lips—Anna felt a rush of satisfaction that was almost as good as her own orgasm.

She'd done that. She'd made Margot feel good. That mattered.

Margot pulled her up, kissed her deeply, then wrapped her arms around her and held on.

"Stay," she murmured against Anna's hair. "Stay the night."

Anna nodded. She didn't want to go home to her empty flat, her cold bed, the letters waiting on her laptop. She wanted this— Margot's warmth, Margot's arms, the simple comfort of another body beside her.

"Okay," she said. "I'll stay."

* * *

Margot fell asleep within minutes. Her arm went heavy across Anna's waist, her breathing slow and even. The room was quiet. Saturday-night traffic filtered up from the street, faint and ordinary.

Anna lay awake.

The sex had been good. She wasn't rearranging the facts. Margot had been attentive, generous, skilled. She'd made Anna come —really come, not the half-hearted thing she'd faked with previous partners.

But the whole time, some part of Anna had been waiting. Waiting for the questions to stop and the instructions to start. For Margot to quit asking *is this okay* and *what do you need* and just... take over. Pin her wrists. Tell her not to move. Fill the space in Anna's head that never stopped evaluating and performing and second-guessing with a single clear voice that said *hold still* and meant it.

That hadn't happened. Margot was careful and kind and she asked because asking was right, and Anna had lain beneath her being well-pleasured and unable to stop thinking for even one second.

That was what the letters described, wasn't it? That was what M. had given Eleanor. A space where thought stopped. Where the constant hum of self-consciousness—*am I doing this right, what should I want, how should I respond*—went quiet, replaced by something simpler. You do what you're told. You hold still. You surrender, and in the surrender, you finally get to stop performing.

Anna hadn't stopped performing tonight. She'd been good— responsive, appreciative, actively participating. She'd been the kind of lover Margot wanted her to be. She'd asked the right questions and made the right sounds and done everything she was supposed to do.

But she hadn't surrendered. She hadn't been able to. There was nothing to surrender *to*.

Margot shifted in her sleep, pulling Anna closer. Her hand spread warm and heavy across Anna's stomach—a gesture of posses-sion, of comfort. Anna should have felt held. Instead she felt the absence of the other kind of holding. The kind that came with commands and expectations and the particular relief of having someone else decide.

She thought about M.'s letters. *I want you to trust me enough to be empty, and to let me fill you.*

She hadn't been empty tonight. She'd been full—full of questions, full of self-consciousness, full of the effort of being a good partner. She'd brought her whole self to bed, and her whole self had been too much.

This isn't fair, she told herself. Margot is wonderful. Margot is kind and generous and she likes you. You're lying in her bed after genuinely good sex and all you can think about is a dead woman who wrote letters a hundred and thirty years ago.

But the thoughts wouldn't stop. They ran in circles, wearing grooves in her mind. The gap between what had happened and what she'd wanted. The impossibility of explaining that gap to Margot without sounding ungrateful, or broken, or obsessed with a fantasy that had nothing to do with reality.

Maybe it was her. Maybe she was the problem. Maybe she'd read too many letters and built up an impossible standard, and now she'd never be satisfied with anything real.

Or maybe she just needed to give it time. It was early. They were still learning each other. You couldn't expect perfect compatibility on the first night. Margot had said she'd done this before—the dynamic Anna was looking for. Maybe she was just being careful, taking it slow, waiting to see what Anna could handle.

Maybe if Anna asked—

But she couldn't imagine asking. Couldn't imagine saying the words out loud. *I want you to stop asking what I want. I want you to tell me what to do. I want to be held down and given orders and made to hold still until you decide I can move.*

Beside her, Margot slept peacefully. One of them had gotten what she needed tonight.

Anna lay still in the dark and waited for morning.

CHAPTER 10

December came to Oxford in shades of grey and gold—grey skies, grey stone, golden light spilling from college windows as the evenings drew in early. The streets filled with students hurrying between libraries, tourists photographing the Christmas markets, locals who had learned long ago to navigate around both.

Anna barely noticed. She was too busy being happy.

It crept up on her, the happiness. She hadn't expected it—hadn't expected any of this, really. The woman who texted her good morning and good night. The dinners that stretched into evenings that stretched into mornings. The particular pleasure of having someone to tell things to, someone who asked about her day and actually listened to the answer.

She and Margot fell into a rhythm. Tuesday nights at Margot's flat—Anna would bring wine, Margot would cook, they'd eat at the counter and talk until it was too late to go home. Friday lunches at the canteen, where Margot would send out something special from the kitchen, a little better than what everyone else was eating, and Anna would pretend not to notice the other staff smiling at them. Sunday afternoons when Margot wasn't working: museums, walks along the river, a disastrous attempt at ice skating that left them both bruised and laughing.

Neither of them had said the word *girlfriend*. But that's what they were. Anna could feel it in the way Margot's colleagues nodded at her now, familiar. In the way Margot had cleared a drawer in her bathroom for Anna's things. In the way Anna's phone lit up with Margot's name and she smiled before she'd decided to.

It was good. It was really good.

If Anna sometimes lay awake after Margot fell asleep, her mind drifting to Victorian letters and a dynamic she couldn't name—well. That was just her brain being difficult. It didn't mean anything.

* * *

"Tell me something I don't know about you," Margot said.

They were lying in bed on a Tuesday night, the remains of dinner abandoned in the kitchen, the lamp casting warm shadows across the ceiling. Margot was propped on one elbow, her free hand drawing absent patterns on Anna's stomach.

"Like what?"

"Anything. Something from before. Your childhood, your terrible teenage years, your first heartbreak. I want to know who you were before I met you."

Anna considered. Her life before Oxford felt distant now—a different person, almost. The quiet girl in the back of the classroom. The teenager who'd preferred the library to parties. The university student who'd fumbled through relationships she didn't really want, trying to figure out why none of it felt right.

"I was very boring," she said. "Genuinely. I didn't have terrible teenage years because I didn't have any teenage years. I just—studied. Read books. Kept my head down."

"Nobody's that boring."

"I was." Anna turned her head to look at Margot. "I think I was waiting for something, even then. I just didn't know what it was. So I filled the time with books and qualifications and work. Things I could control."

"And now?" Margot's hand stilled on her stomach. "Have you found what you were waiting for?"

The question hung in the air. Anna knew what Margot wanted her to say. *Yes. You. I was waiting for you.*

"I'm getting closer," she said instead. It was true. It just wasn't the whole truth.

Margot smiled and leaned down to kiss her. "I'll take closer," she murmured against Anna's lips. "We've got time."

* * *

At work, Anna was preparing her proposal.

The Ashworth letters deserved proper recognition. She'd spent weeks now building the case—provenance documentation, historical context, comparisons to other significant finds. Victorian sapphic correspondence was rare; correspondence this explicit, this sustained, was rarer still. With the right framing, it could be a significant publication. It could establish her reputation.

Dr. Fitzwilliam had been cautiously encouraging. "It's certainly unusual material," she'd said, reviewing Anna's preliminary notes. "The connection to the textile collection is intriguing. Have you considered approaching it as a material culture study? The letters and the dress together—the embodied aspects of the relationship— that's the angle that would interest the journals."

The embodied aspects. Anna had nodded and taken notes and not mentioned that she'd spent more time thinking about those embodied aspects than was strictly professional.

She worked on the proposal in the mornings, before Marcus arrived, when the conservation room was quiet and she could spread her transcriptions across the bench without anyone asking questions. The letters had become so familiar now that she could recite passages from memory. M.'s measured voice, Eleanor's passionate responses.

The careful architecture of their relationship, built through words and fabric and Thursday afternoons.

You ask why I want what I want, Eleanor had written. *I do not know how to answer except to say that when I am with you, I am more myself than I have ever been anywhere else.*

Anna understood that now. The paradox of it—becoming more yourself by giving yourself away. It made a kind of sense that nothing else in her life had ever made.

She just wished she could find it with someone who was still alive.

* * *

On Friday, Margot texted her mid-morning: *Ashmolean tomorrow? They've got a new exhibition. Japanese textiles.*

Anna smiled at her phone. Margot had been making an effort lately to suggest activities related to Anna's interests—museums, exhibitions, a lecture on medieval manuscripts that had bored Margot senseless but that she'd attended anyway, asking questions afterward that showed she'd actually been paying attention.

Perfect, Anna typed back. *What time?*

11? Then lunch after. I know a place.

Anna liked that Margot always knew a place. Liked the confidence of it, the easy assumption that she could navigate the world and find the best version of whatever they needed. It was one of the things that had drawn her in the first place—that quality of competence, of being in charge.

She just wished it extended further. Into other rooms. Other contexts.

But that wasn't fair. Margot was who she was. And who she was, was lovely.

See you then, Anna sent, and put her phone away, and tried to focus on the water-damaged manuscript in front of her.

* * *

The Ashmolean was quiet on Saturday morning, the galleries half-empty, their footsteps echoing on the marble floors. The Japanese textile exhibition was small but exquisite—centuries-old kimonos displayed in climate-controlled cases, their silk still vibrant, their embroidery still precise.

Anna moved through the gallery slowly, studying each piece with the attention she'd bring to any historical textile. The construction techniques. The dye methods. The wear patterns that showed how these garments had been used, stored, valued.

Margot followed, patient and curious. She asked questions—good questions, the kind that showed she was thinking about what she was seeing rather than just looking.

"What's the significance of this pattern?" she asked, pointing to a kimono covered in stylized waves. "Is it just decorative, or does it mean something?"

"Waves usually represent strength and resilience," Anna said. "The ability to adapt to change. And they're associated with luck—fishermen's families would use wave patterns to wish for safe returns."

"So the clothes carry meaning. Messages."

"Almost always. Clothing is never just cloth. It's communication—who you are, who you want to be, what you want other people to see." Anna paused, looking at the waves. "Or what you want to hide."

Margot was quiet for a moment. Then: "Like your dress. The green one, with the hidden alterations."

Anna turned to look at her. She hadn't expected Margot to make the connection—hadn't expected her to remember the details.

"Yes," she said. "Exactly like that."

"A message only two people could read."

"Yes."

Margot nodded slowly, her eyes still on the kimono. "That's beautiful," she said. "And a little bit sad. Having to hide it like that. Having to code everything."

"They didn't have a choice. It was that or nothing."

"I know." Margot reached out and took Anna's hand, lacing their fingers together. "I'm glad we don't have to hide. You and me. I'm glad we can just—be."

Anna squeezed her hand. She was glad too.

But some part of her—small, shameful, impossible to silence— thought about the green silk dress. About the thrill of a secret shared in plain sight. About Eleanor sitting at dinner with fourteen people, feeling M.'s work pressed against her ribs, and knowing that only she and M. understood what it meant.

There was something in the hiding. Something in the code. Something that got lost when you could just—be.

She didn't say any of this. She held Margot's hand and watched the waves on the silk and let the thought sit where it was.

* * *

Lunch was at a small restaurant Margot knew, tucked down a side street near the covered market. The food was Middle Eastern, rich with spices, and Margot ordered for both of them without asking, a habit Anna had noticed and never commented on.

She liked it when Margot ordered for her. Liked the small abdication of choice. It was such a tiny thing, meaningless really, but it scratched an itch she couldn't name.

"So," Margot said, tearing off a piece of flatbread and dipping it in hummus. "Christmas. What are your plans?"

"My parents' place in Surrey. Same as every year." Anna made a face. "Three days of my mother asking when I'm going to find someone, my father pretending not to hear, and my brother's children running around screaming."

"When you're going to find someone?" Margot's eyebrow rose. "Should I be offended?"

"She doesn't know about you. About—us." Anna hesitated. "I haven't told them."

"Because I'm a woman?"

"No—they know I date women. They've known for years." Anna pushed her food around her plate. "I just—I don't tell them things. Generally. We're not close like that."

Margot was quiet for a moment, studying her. "Would you want to be? Close like that?"

"I don't know. Maybe. Sometimes." Anna sighed. "It's complicated. They love me, I think, in their way. They just don't—see me. They see the daughter they expected to have, and I've never quite matched up."

"The quiet girl in the back of the classroom."

"Exactly. They wanted someone brighter. More present. More —" She waved her hand vaguely. "More."

Margot reached across the table and caught her hand. "You're plenty," she said. "You know that, right? You're not less than anyone."

Anna felt her throat tighten. Nobody said things like that to her. Nobody had ever said things like that to her.

"Thank you," she managed.

"I mean it." Margot's thumb traced circles on her palm. "You're one of the most interesting people I've ever met. The way your mind works. The things you notice. The way you care about these old objects, these old stories—it's not boring, Anna. It's beautiful. You're beautiful."

Anna didn't know what to say. She felt seen, suddenly, in a way that was almost uncomfortable. Margot was looking at her like she mattered, like she was worth paying attention to, and it was everything Anna had ever wanted and also somehow not quite enough.

What was wrong with her? Why couldn't she just accept this?

"You're going to make me cry in a restaurant," she said, trying to deflect.

"I've seen worse." But Margot let her hand go, gave her space. "Anyway. Christmas. If you wanted—I mean, you probably don't, it's early, and I know we haven't—" She stopped, started again. "My sister hosts Christmas Eve. In London. It's chaos, there are about a hundred children, and the food is terrible because she insists on doing it herself instead of letting me help. But if you wanted to come, before you go to Surrey. You'd be welcome."

Anna looked at her across the table. Margot, who was confident about everything, suddenly uncertain. Offering something that mattered. Waiting to see if Anna would take it.

"Yes," Anna said. "I'd like that."

Margot's smile was worth every complication.

* * *

That night, alone in her flat, Anna opened the textile repository's digital archive and looked at her photographs of the dress.

She'd requested permission to bring it to her own conservation lab. The paperwork had been approved; she could collect it next week. The prospect should have excited her—a chance to examine the alterations properly, to document everything, to understand exactly how M. had constructed this secret—but instead she felt a strange melancholy.

The dress had been waiting for sixty years. Folded in tissue paper, stored in climate-controlled darkness, untouched and unremembered. The woman who'd worn it, who'd felt its hidden architecture against her body, had been dead for eighty years. The woman who'd made it—M., whose full name Anna still didn't know—had probably died even earlier.

Everything ended. That was the lesson of archives, of conservation, of old things preserved in careful conditions. You could keep the objects, but you couldn't keep the people. You could save the letters, but you couldn't save the love.

Anna thought about Margot. About Christmas Eve with her sister's family. About the life that was taking shape in front of her— real, present, possible.

She thought about M., a century dead, whose voice she knew better than her own mother's.

It wasn't fair to Margot, this comparison. It wasn't fair to any of them—not to Margot, not to Eleanor, not to M., not to Anna herself. The letters were a highlight reel, not a life. M. had probably been annoying sometimes. Probably snored, or forgot appointments, or said the wrong thing at the wrong moment. No relationship was as perfect as the letters made it seem.

Anna knew this. She knew it intellectually, knew it professionally. She worked with archives; she understood that documents were partial, selective, incomplete. The past was always edited.

But knowing didn't stop the wanting. Knowing didn't make Margot's voice sound like M.'s, or Margot's hands feel like the hands that had sewn hidden boning into green silk. Knowing didn't fill the gap between what Anna had and what she craved.

She closed the photograph and opened her transcription file instead. Found the passage she kept returning to, the one that wouldn't let her go:

I want you to trust me enough to be empty, and to let me fill you.

She read the passage three times, then closed her laptop and went to bed. In the morning she'd text Margot. Tonight she stared at the ceiling and let the wanting be what it was.

CHAPTER 11

It happened on a Tuesday, the week before Christmas.

Anna was at Margot's flat, sitting at the kitchen counter while Margot cooked. This had become their ritual—Anna with a glass of wine, watching Margot move through the kitchen, offering to help and being waved away. Margot didn't like other people in her workspace. She'd been clear about that from the start.

"Can you pass me the—" Margot turned, gesturing toward the counter where Anna sat. "The olive oil. Behind you."

Anna reached for it, but her sleeve caught on her wine glass. The glass tipped, rolled toward the edge of the counter—

"Don't move."

Margot's voice was sharp, commanding. The voice she used in her kitchen when something was about to go wrong—a pan overheating, a knife slipping, a situation requiring immediate control.

Anna froze.

Not the normal freeze of someone startled. Something deeper. Her whole body went still, her breath catching, her hands stopping exactly where they were. The wine glass rolled off the counter and shattered on the floor, but Anna didn't flinch. Didn't move. Didn't do anything except stay exactly, precisely where Margot's voice had fixed her.

Margot crossed the kitchen in two strides, avoiding the broken glass, and caught Anna's arm. "You okay? Did any of it get you?"

"I'm fine." Anna's voice came out strange. Distant. She was still frozen, she realized—still holding the position Margot's command had put her in.

She made herself move. Lowered her hands. Looked down at the shattered glass and the spreading pool of red wine on Margot's kitchen floor.

"I'm so sorry—let me clean it up—"

"Stay there. There's glass everywhere. I'll get the dustpan."

Anna stayed. She watched Margot fetch the dustpan and brush, sweep up the broken glass, mop up the wine with kitchen towel.

Margot hadn't noticed. Had she? It had been a split second, a reflex, nothing remarkable. Anyone would have frozen when someone shouted at them. It didn't mean anything.

But when Margot straightened up, dustpan in hand, she was looking at Anna with an expression Anna couldn't quite read.

"You really don't move when someone tells you not to," she said. "Do you?"

Anna's looked away. "I—it was just—you startled me."

"Mmm." Margot deposited the broken glass in the bin and came back to where Anna sat. She leaned against the counter, close but not touching, her eyes still thoughtful. "That wasn't startled. Startled is flinching. Jumping. You went completely still. Like you were waiting for the next instruction."

Anna didn't know what to say.

"It's okay," Margot said, more gently. "I'm not criticizing. I just —I noticed, that's all."

"Noticed what?"

"That you liked it." Margot's voice was soft, curious. "The command. The being told. You liked it."

Anna couldn't deny it. Couldn't make herself lie, not about this, not to Margot who was looking at her with such careful attention.

"Yes," she whispered. "I liked it."

Margot nodded slowly. She reached out and tucked a strand of hair behind Anna's ear—a tender gesture, nothing commanding about it—and said, "Good to know."

Then she went back to cooking, and Anna sat at the counter still buzzing from two words in a sharp voice, and wondered what was going to happen next.

* * *

They ate dinner. They talked about normal things—Margot's plans for the canteen's Christmas menu, Anna's progress on the proposal, the logistics of Christmas Eve at Margot's sister's house. The broken wine glass wasn't mentioned again.

The air between them was different now. Anna could feel Margot working something out behind her eyes.

After dinner, they moved to the sofa. Margot poured them both whisky—"for the shock," she said, with a wry smile that suggested she knew the shock had nothing to do with broken glass—and they sat close together in the lamplight, not quite touching.

"Can I ask you something?" Margot said.

"Yes."

"The letters. The dynamic you told me about—the dressmaker and the lady. Is that what you want? What they had?"

"I—some of it. Parts of it."

"Which parts?"

She couldn't look at Margot while she answered. Stared at her whisky instead, at the amber light catching in the glass.

"The structure," she said slowly. "The—being told what to do. Having someone else decide. Not having to—" She stopped, frustrated with her own inability to articulate it. "It's like my brain never stops, you know? Always thinking, analyzing, second-guessing. And when someone tells me what to do—really tells me, with authority—it just... stops. For a second. Everything goes quiet."

Margot was quiet for a moment. Then she set her whisky down on the side table and turned toward Anna, her expression intent.

"Look at me," she said.

It wasn't the sharp command from the kitchen. It was softer, more deliberate—a test rather than a reflex. But it had the same weight behind it, the same expectation of compliance.

Anna looked at her.

"Good." Margot's voice was warm with approval. "Now put your glass down."

Anna set her whisky beside Margot's on the side table.

"Come here."

Anna moved closer, until their knees were touching.

"Closer."

She shifted into Margot's lap, straddling her thighs, suddenly breathless. Margot's hands came up to rest on her hips—steadying, possessive.

"Is your brain quiet now?" Margot asked.

Anna nodded. She couldn't speak. The noise that usually filled her head—the constant analysis, the second-guessing, the running commentary on her own performance—had gone silent. There was only this: Margot's hands on her hips, Margot's eyes holding hers, the simple clarity of having been told where to be and being there.

"I thought so." Margot's thumbs traced circles on Anna's hipbones, slow and deliberate. "You should have told me. That this is what you needed."

"I didn't know how."

"You're telling me now." Margot's hands slid up Anna's sides, over her ribs, came to rest just below her breasts. "Your body's telling me. You're shaking."

She was. She hadn't noticed, but she was trembling—not from cold, not from fear, but from something else entirely. Relief, maybe. Recognition. The feeling of finally, finally being seen.

"Take off your shirt," Margot said.

Anna reached for the hem with hands that shook. Pulled it over her head, dropped it somewhere behind her. The air was cool on her bare skin. She was wearing a plain cotton bra, nothing special, but the way Margot looked at her made her feel like she was wearing silk.

"Beautiful," Margot murmured. "Now hold still. Don't move until I tell you."

Anna held still.

Margot's hands explored her—slowly, deliberately, like she was mapping terrain. She traced the curve of Anna's waist, the line of her collarbone, the soft skin inside her elbows. She didn't go anywhere obvious, didn't touch her breasts or reach between her legs. She just... looked. Touched. Catalogued.

Anna had never felt so exposed. So completely, exquisitely *seen*.

"You're very responsive," Margot observed. Her finger traced Anna's lower lip, and Anna's mouth parted automatically. "You're holding so still for me. That takes effort, doesn't it?"

"Yes." The word came out rough.

"But you like the effort."

"Yes."

"Good girl."

The words hit Anna like a physical blow. Her whole body shuddered, her eyes fluttering closed despite the instruction to hold still. *Good girl.* Nobody had ever—she had never—

"Eyes open," Margot said, and Anna's eyes flew open. "I want you to see what I'm doing to you. I want you to watch."

"Yes."

"Yes, what?"

Anna didn't know what Margot wanted. Didn't know the script. But something rose up in her, instinctive, and she heard herself say: "Yes. Please."

Margot's smile was slow and warm and devastating. "There you are," she said softly. "There's my girl."

And then she pulled Anna down and kissed her, and Anna stopped thinking about anything at all, which was the whole point.

* * *

They made it to the bedroom eventually. Anna wasn't sure how—she remembered being lifted, carried, her legs wrapped around Margot's waist, and then the softness of the bed beneath her back and Margot above her, still giving commands.

"Hands above your head."

Anna put her hands above her head.

"Keep them there. Don't move them."

Anna gripped the headboard and didn't move them.

Margot undressed her slowly, methodically, narrating as she went. "I'm going to take off your bra now. Then your jeans. Then I'm going to look at you for as long as I want, and you're going to let me." Each statement a small command, a small surrender. Anna lay beneath her and gave herself over to it, let Margot arrange her and position her and decide what happened next.

It was nothing like their first time. That had been good—genuinely good—but this was something else entirely. This was the thing Anna had been reaching for, the shape she'd been trying to find in the dark. Margot's voice, calm and certain, telling her what to do. The relief of not having to decide. The exquisite pleasure of being held in place by nothing but words and expectation.

"You're so wet," Margot said, her fingers sliding between Anna's legs. "Just from being told what to do. Just from holding still for me."

Anna made a sound—half moan, half sob. She was beyond words now, beyond anything except sensation and obedience.

"I'm going to make you come," Margot told her. "And you're going to keep your hands where they are. You're going to hold still and let me, and you're not going to look away from me. Understand?"

"Yes." It came out broken. "Yes, please, yes—"

Margot's fingers slid inside her, and her thumb found Anna's clit, and she set a rhythm that was relentless and perfect and exactly what Anna needed. Anna's hips tried to rise, tried to chase the sensation, but Margot's free hand pressed flat against her stomach—the same gesture from before, but intentional now, deliberate—and held her down.

"I said hold still."

Anna held still. Her body screamed to move, to arch, to participate, but she held still because Margot had told her to, and the effort of the obedience was itself a kind of pleasure, a kind of surrender that went deeper than anything physical.

"That's it," Margot murmured. "That's my good girl. Let me take you there. Let me—"

Anna came. The orgasm crashed through her like a wave, like a wall, like something too big for her body to contain. She cried out —couldn't help it, couldn't hold that in even if everything else was held perfectly still—and Margot stayed with her through all of it, her fingers working, her voice murmuring praise, *that's it, good girl, there you go, that's my girl—*

When it finally ebbed, Anna was crying.

She didn't know when she'd started. The tears were just there, streaming down her temples, soaking into her hair. She wasn't sad— wasn't anything she could name—just overwhelmed, cracked open, undone.

"Hey." Margot's voice was soft now, all the command gone out of it. She gathered Anna into her arms, pulled her close, stroked her hair. "Hey. I've got you. You're okay."

"I know." Anna's voice was thick with tears. "I know. I'm not —it's not bad. It's just—"

"A lot."

"Yes." She pressed her face into Margot's shoulder. "It's a lot."

Margot held her while she cried. Didn't ask questions, didn't demand explanations, just held her and stroked her hair and let her fall apart. When the tears finally slowed, she pressed a kiss to Anna's forehead and said, "You did so well. You were perfect."

Perfect. The word settled into Anna's chest like a stone, like a gift. She had been perfect. Margot had said so.

"Can we—" Anna swallowed. "Can you—I want to—" She couldn't find the words. Couldn't explain that she needed to give something back, needed to make Margot feel even a fraction of what she'd just experienced.

"Later." Margot's arms tightened around her. "Right now I just want to hold you. Is that okay?"

Anna nodded against her shoulder. It was more than okay. It was everything.

———

Later—much later, after they'd both recovered, after Anna had reciprocated with enthusiasm if not expertise—they lay tangled together in Margot's bed, the sheets a wreck around them.

"So," Margot said. Her fingers were tracing lazy patterns on Anna's shoulder. "That was different."

"Good different?"

"Very good different." Margot turned her head to look at Anna. "You should have told me sooner. That this is what you needed."

"I didn't—" Anna hesitated. "I didn't know if you'd want to. If it was too much to ask."

"Anna." Margot's voice was gently exasperated. "I told you the first time we had coffee that I'd done this before. That I'd been on the giving end. Did you think I was lying?"

"No. I just—" Anna struggled to explain. "I didn't want to pressure you. To make you be something you weren't. I wanted you to want it too, not just do it because I asked."

"I do want it." Margot propped herself up on one elbow, looking down at Anna with serious eyes. "Not all the time—I'm not always in that headspace, and sometimes I just want regular sex, you know? But when it works, when both people are in it—" She smiled.

"That was incredible. Watching you let go like that. Feeling you trust me enough to fall apart. That's not a burden, Anna. That's a gift."

Anna felt tears prick at her eyes again. She blinked them back. "I've never—no one's ever—"

"I know." Margot leaned down and kissed her softly. "But I'm here now. And I want to learn you. All of you. The parts you show everyone and the parts you've been hiding."

Anna pulled her down and kissed her back, trying to pour everything she couldn't say into it. Gratitude. Hope. The terrifying, exhilarating sense that maybe—maybe—she had finally found what she'd been looking for.

Margot could be this. Anna let the thought settle without interrogating it. She'd interrogated enough things lately.

She should have asked sooner. She should have trusted Margot with this from the beginning.

But she was asking now. And Margot was answering. And maybe that was enough.

Anna fell asleep in Margot's arms, more content than she'd been in months, and didn't dream of the dressmaker at all.

CHAPTER 12

Christmas Eve at Margot's sister's house was exactly the chaos Margot had promised: too many people in too small a space, children careening between rooms, food that was well-intentioned but bland. Anna spent an hour being interviewed by Margot's nieces—seven and nine, fiercely opinionated about Disney princesses—and found she didn't mind. They didn't expect her to be interesting. They just wanted someone to listen, and listening was the thing she was best at.

"You're good with them," Margot said afterward, as they walked to the Tube through holiday-empty streets. "I thought you'd be overwhelmed."

"I was," Anna said. "But they're easy to be around. Nobody under ten has ever accused me of being distant."

Margot laughed and took her hand. Their breath misted in the cold. Anna thought about the evening—the noise, the warmth, the way Margot's family had folded her in without ceremony, as if her presence had been assumed. It had been good. She'd felt welcome.

So why had she spent the whole evening holding her breath?

* * *

The new year came quietly. Anna spent Christmas in Surrey with her parents—three days of her mother's polite disappointment and her father's careful silence—and came back to Oxford feeling scraped out.

Margot met her at the station and kissed her on the platform in front of everyone. Something in Anna's chest unclenched.

"Bad?" Margot asked, reading her face.

"Not bad. I'm glad to be back."

"Come on." Margot took her bag. "I'm taking you home and feeding you and you don't have to talk about any of it."

That night, in Margot's bed, things were different. Margot had clearly been thinking about their last time together—the wine glass, the commands, the sofa. She was more deliberate now, more intentional. She gave Anna instructions ("Hands here." "Don't move." "Look at me.") with a confidence that suggested she'd been practicing, working out the voice.

And Anna responded. She felt her body soften when Margot told her what to do. Let herself be directed. It worked, mostly.

But Margot kept breaking the surface. "Is this okay?" after a command. "Tell me what you're feeling" when Anna was sinking into the quiet. The questions pulled her back—not all the way, but far enough. Far enough to remind her that she was supposed to have answers. That Margot was waiting for her to participate in her own direction.

Anna said "yes" and "good" and "more." When she came, the orgasm was real. The pleasure was real.

"That was good, right?" Margot said afterward, holding her close.

"That was good," Anna said, and it wasn't a lie, and it wasn't the whole truth, and the space between those two things was where she lived now.

* * *

January was cold and bright. Anna threw herself into the proposal —the letters transcribed and annotated, the argument for their significance carefully built. Dr. Fitzwilliam gave preliminary approval. If all went well, the collection would be formally catalogued by spring.

She should have been excited. Instead, she kept returning to the letters themselves. Not for research—she had them memorized by now—but for M.'s voice.

You will wear the green silk to the Harcourt dinner, M. had written. *You will think of me when you dress, when you feel the bones against your ribs. You will sit through courses and conversation knowing what lies beneath. And when you return home—alone, as you must—you will write to me at once. You will tell me everything: how it felt to carry our secret among people who could not see it. How you sat, how you breathed, how you endured. I will not be there. But I will be holding you all the same.*

The certainty of it. The way M. didn't ask Eleanor what she wanted. The way M. decided, and expected, and Eleanor leaned into the structure like leaning against a wall that would hold.

Margot didn't work that way. Margot treated their dynamic like a collaboration, each of them contributing. Anna knew this was better. She knew it the way she knew academic things—clearly, completely, from the outside.

* * *

On a Friday night in late January, Margot tried something new.

She'd set up the bedroom: candles, the overhead light off, music from her phone. She was waiting by the bed with a silk scarf in her hands.

"I thought we could try something," she said. "If you want. No pressure."

Anna's heart beat faster. "I want to try."

Margot smiled. "Give me your hands."

She wrapped the scarf around Anna's wrists—loosely, carefully, checking the fit. "Too tight?"

"No."

"You can get out whenever you need to. Just twist and pull. I'm not really restraining you. It's—*symbolic*. Okay?"

"Okay."

Margot tied her hands to the headboard and stepped back to look. Her expression was warm, a little playful.

"God, Anna. You look incredible."

Anna tried to sink into it. The bound hands, the exposure, the sense of being displayed. This was what she wanted. The surrender. The quiet.

But the scarf was loose. She could feel how easily she could undo it. The knot sat on her wrists like a suggestion, not a fact, and her mind kept feeling the gap between what was happening and what she'd imagined.

The green silk dress hadn't been symbolic. The boning along Eleanor's ribs had been real, physical, inescapable. She couldn't have undone it with a twist of her wrist. The constraint had been actual, not performative—a structure she lived inside, not a game she could end at any moment.

She pushed the thought away. She was here, with Margot, who had lit candles and bought a scarf and was looking at her like she was something worth having.

"Please," Anna said, because Margot was waiting for it.

Margot climbed onto the bed, straddled Anna's hips. Ran her hands up Anna's bound arms, leaned down to kiss her.

"I've been thinking about this all week," she murmured against Anna's mouth. "About having you like this. About all the things I want to do to you."

"Tell me." Anna's voice came out rougher than she intended. "Tell me what you want to do."

"I want to make you beg." Margot's smile was wicked, playful. "I want to tease you until you're desperate. I want to hear you ask for it."

She wanted Anna to *ask*. Even now, even with Anna's hands tied above her head, Margot wanted her to participate. To verbalize. To be an active partner in her own submission.

M. wouldn't have wanted that. M. would have decided when Anna was allowed to come and told her, not waited for her to beg. The begging would have been a failure of discipline, not a goal.

Anna pushed the thought away. She was here, with Margot, who was trying so hard to give her what she needed. Who had lit candles and bought a silk scarf and was looking at her with such desire.

"Please," she said, because that was what Margot wanted to hear.

Margot's smile widened. She began kissing her way down Anna's body. Her mouth was skilled and warm and generous. She edged Anna until Anna was shaking, then let her come, and Anna cried out and arched and the orgasm was real and her body convulsed against the silk and none of it was fake.

* * *

The sex was good. It was always good—Margot was skilled and attentive and genuinely cared about Anna's pleasure. She edged Anna until she was shaking, then finally let her come, and Anna cried out and arched against her bonds and performed all the responses that the situation seemed to require.

Afterward Margot untied her wrists, rubbed them gently, checked for marks.

"How was that? Did it work for you?"

"That was amazing," Anna said, and smiled, and Margot looked pleased but also—searching. Uncertain.

"You seemed a little distant at the end. Were you okay?"

Anna's stomach tightened. Margot had noticed. She always noticed.

"Just overwhelmed. In a good way."

Margot studied her for a long moment. "Okay. As long as you're okay."

"Better than okay." Anna buried her face in Margot's shoulder so she wouldn't have to hold eye contact. "Thank you. For trying that."

"I want to figure this out," Margot said. "What works for us. We're still learning."

"Still learning," Anna echoed.

*　*　*

Over the next few weeks, Margot kept experimenting. More commands one night. Fewer the next. A proper blindfold to replace the scarf. Stricter one evening, softer the following. She was paying attention, adjusting, doing her best.

And Anna appreciated it. She did. The effort Margot was putting in, the care, the willingness to try things that didn't come naturally to her. Margot wasn't pretending to be something she wasn't—she was stretching, adapting, trying to meet Anna where she was.

But the stretching was visible. That was the problem. Anna could see the seams, could feel Margot thinking about what to do next, could sense the improvisation behind every command. It wasn't instinct; it was effort. Margot was playing a role, playing it well, but playing it nonetheless.

M. hadn't played a role. M. had simply *been* what she was—a woman who gave orders and expected them to be followed, whose authority came from somewhere deep and unquestionable. Reading her letters, Anna had never once felt like M. was performing dominance. It had simply been who she was.

Margot's dominance was a gift she was giving Anna. M.'s dominance had been a gift she was letting Eleanor receive.

The distinction mattered. Anna didn't know how to explain why, but it mattered.

So she performed. Gratitude, pleasure, satisfaction. She told Margot how good it was, how much she appreciated her, how lucky she felt. And it was true—all of it was true. She *was* grateful. She *did* appreciate Margot's effort. She *was* lucky to have found someone willing to try.

It just wasn't enough. And she hated herself for that—for being the kind of person who could have something good and still want something else.

* * *

One night in early February, Anna woke to find Margot watching her.

Three in the morning, maybe four. Dark room, streetlight glow through the curtains. Margot on her side, propped on one elbow, eyes fixed on Anna's face.

"Hey," Anna said. "What's wrong?"

"Nothing. Just woke up."

"How long have you been watching me?"

"A while." A pause. "You look different asleep. More relaxed. Like you're not—" She stopped.

"Not what?"

Margot was quiet for a long time. Anna couldn't see her expression in the dark.

"Never mind," Margot said. "Go back to sleep."

She rolled over. Anna stared at the curve of her back and felt something crack open in her chest—not the pleasant kind of opening, but the kind that lets cold air in.

Margot knew. Not the specifics, maybe—not the letters, not M., not the precise shape of what was missing. But she knew something was wrong. She'd been lying in the dark watching Anna sleep, trying to find the woman underneath the performance.

Anna should say something. Should tell whatever truth she could assemble. But what was the truth? *You're wonderful and you're not enough.* She couldn't say that. Couldn't find a version of it that wasn't an accusation.

She curled against Margot's back and put an arm around her and said nothing.

Margot's hand found hers. Squeezed. Didn't let go.

They lay like that until morning. Neither of them slept. Neither of them said so.

CHAPTER 13

The idea came to her on a Thursday afternoon.

Anna was at her workbench, supposedly reviewing the final draft of her proposal, but her mind kept drifting. To Margot. To the growing distance between them that neither of them had named. To the impossible task of explaining what she wanted when she couldn't find the words.

She'd tried, hadn't she? She'd told Margot about the letters, about the dynamic, about the way her brain went quiet when someone gave her commands. Margot had listened. Had tried. Was still trying.

But trying wasn't the same as understanding.

Anna stared at the transcriptions spread across her desk—M.'s careful handwriting rendered into digital text, Eleanor's passionate responses preserved in neat paragraphs. These women had known how to talk to each other. Had built a language together, a vocabulary of desire that communicated everything Anna couldn't seem to say.

What if she let the letters speak for her?

She started gathering the pages before she'd finished the thought.

She didn't know what else to do.

* * *

She brought the transcriptions to Margot's flat on Friday night.

"I want to show you something," she said, after dinner, after wine, after they'd settled onto the sofa in their usual positions. "The letters I've been working on. I've never let you read them properly—just told you about them. But I think—" She hesitated. "I think you should see them. So you can understand what I've been... what they mean to me."

Margot looked at her for a long moment. Something flickered across her face—caution, maybe. Wariness. But she nodded and took the folder Anna offered.

"Okay," she said. "I'd like to understand."

She began to read.

Anna watched her. Watched her eyes move across the pages, her expression shifting as she absorbed M.'s words. The early letters first—the careful establishment of the dynamic, the first commands, Eleanor's tentative acceptance. Then the middle period—the deepening intimacy, the green silk dress, the elaborate rituals they'd built together. Then the later letters—the passion, the devotion, the absolute certainty of two people who had found exactly what they needed in each other.

Margot read slowly, carefully. She didn't speak. Didn't look up. Just turned the pages, one after another, absorbing.

Anna sat across from her on the sofa and waited. Any moment now, Margot would look up with recognition in her eyes. She'd say *I understand now* or *I see what you need* or *let me try again*. The letters would do what Anna couldn't—they'd communicate the shape of her desire in language precise enough to be acted upon.

Margot reached the end. Set down the last page. Looked up.

Anna saw her face and felt something cold settle in her stomach.

"These are remarkable," Margot said. Her voice was careful. Controlled. "I can see why they're significant. For your work. For the historical record."

"But?"

"But nothing." Margot set the folder on the coffee table. Her movements were precise, deliberate. "They're beautiful. The relationship they describe—it's clear these women loved each other very much."

She wasn't saying what Anna needed her to say. She was treating the letters like documents—interesting, moving, historically significant—not like instructions. Not like a map.

"Margot." Anna heard the desperation in her own voice. "That's not—I didn't show them to you for the history. I showed them because—"

"Because you wanted me to see what you want." Margot's voice was quiet. "What you've been wanting. What I haven't been giving you."

The words hung in the air. Anna couldn't deny them.

"Yes," she whispered. "I thought if you read them, you'd understand—"

"I do understand." Margot stood up. Walked to the window. Her back was to Anna, her shoulders tight. "I understand that you've been comparing me to a dead woman for months. That every time we're together, you're checking to see if I match up to a relationship that ended a hundred and thirty years ago. That you couldn't just *tell* me what you needed—you had to give me a script someone else wrote."

"That's not—"

"Isn't it?" Margot turned. Her face was calm, but her eyes were bright with something Anna couldn't name. "What did you think would happen, Anna? That I'd read these letters and suddenly become her? That I'd start speaking in Victorian prose and issuing commands from on high?"

"No, I—" Anna's throat was closing up. "I just wanted you to see. What it could be. What I've been trying to explain—"

"You haven't been trying to explain anything." Margot's voice cracked on the last word. "You've been waiting. Waiting for me to figure it out on my own, to magically become what you wanted without you having to ask. And when I didn't—when I couldn't—you gave me someone else's words instead of finding your own."

Anna had no defence. Everything Margot was saying was true.

"I'm sorry," she said. It came out small, inadequate. "I didn't know how else—"

"You could have talked to me." Margot's voice was tired now, the anger draining into something worse. "You could have said 'this is what I need, specifically, in detail, in your own words.' You could have trusted me enough to be honest instead of hoping I'd read your mind—or read your historical documents and extrapolate."

"I was afraid."

"Of what?"

"Of asking for something you couldn't give. Of making you feel like you weren't enough." Anna felt tears spilling down her cheeks. "Of being too much. Too complicated. Too broken."

Margot was silent for a long moment. When she spoke again, her voice was very quiet.

"I need some time," she said. "To think about this. About what it means."

"Margot—"

"Please." Margot held up a hand. "I'm not—I'm not ending anything. I just need to think. And I can't do that with you here, looking at me like that. Can you give me that? A few days?"

Anna nodded. She couldn't speak.

She gathered the letters—her damning evidence, her failed shortcut—and let herself out of Margot's flat. The door clicked shut behind her.

The walk home was cold and dark and very long.

CHAPTER 14

Two days of silence.

Anna checked her phone constantly—in the morning when she woke, during breaks at work, in the evening before bed. Nothing. No messages, no missed calls, no indication that Margot was thinking about her at all.

She knew she should give Margot space. That was what Margot had asked for, and Anna owed her at least that much. But her mind wouldn't stop spinning—replaying the conversation, dissecting every word, cataloguing all the ways she'd failed.

You've been comparing me to a dead woman for months.

You couldn't just tell me what you needed.

You gave me someone else's words instead of finding your own.

All true. All undeniable. Anna had done exactly what Margot accused her of, and she didn't have a defence. She'd been so certain that showing Margot the letters would help—would communicate what she couldn't say, would build a bridge between them. Instead, she'd revealed the depth of her betrayal. She'd been in love with a ghost, and she'd let Margot compete with it without even telling her the rules of the game.

On the third morning, her phone buzzed.

Margot: *Can we talk? Your place, if that's okay. Tonight.*

Anna stared at the message. Her place. They never went to her place—it was small, bare, impersonal. A space she slept in rather than lived in. Margot's flat was where they spent their time, with its warm light and worn leather and shelves full of books.

The choice of location felt significant. Pointed.

Of course, she typed back. *7pm?*

See you then.

No kiss. No emoji. No warmth.

Anna set down her phone and tried to breathe.

* * *

She spent the afternoon cleaning her flat—not because it was dirty, but because she needed something to do with her hands. She scrubbed the kitchen counter, organized her bookshelf, changed her sheets even though they didn't need changing. The activity kept the panic at bay, barely.

At six-thirty, she stood in the middle of her living room and looked around with Margot's eyes.

The flat was clean now, but it was still empty. White walls, beige carpet, furniture that had come with the rental. The only personal touches were her books—stacked on every surface, overflowing from the single bookshelf—and her laptop, open on the small desk by the window. No art on the walls. No plants. No photographs.

Sarah's old room stood empty behind a closed door. Eight months since her flatmate had moved out, and Anna still hadn't replaced her. Hadn't even considered it. She'd liked the solitude, the quiet, the space to be alone with her thoughts and her letters.

Now the solitude felt like an accusation. *This is who you are,* the empty flat said. *This is what you've built. A life with no room for anyone else.*

The buzzer rang.

She let Margot in, listened to her footsteps on the stairs, opened the door before she could knock.

Margot looked tired. That was the first thing Anna noticed—the shadows under her eyes, the tension in her shoulders. She wasn't wearing her usual confidence like armour. She looked worn down, uncertain. Human.

"Hi," Anna said.

"Hi."

They stood in the doorway for an awkward moment. Then Anna stepped back, and Margot came in, and the door closed behind her with a click that sounded too loud in the quiet.

Margot looked around the flat. Anna watched her take it in—the bareness, the impersonality, the absence of anything that might suggest who lived here.

"This is the first time I've been here," Margot said. "In all these months."

"I know. I'm sorry—it's not much—"

"Don't apologize." Margot's voice was flat. "It makes sense, actually. That you'd want to be at my place instead of here. There's nothing of you here."

The words landed like a blow. Anna didn't know how to respond.

"Can I sit down?" Margot asked.

"Of course. Yes. Can I get you—tea, or—"

"No. Thank you." Margot sat on the edge of the sofa—the only seating in the room besides a desk chair. She didn't lean back, didn't make herself comfortable. She sat like someone who wasn't planning to stay long.

Anna sat at the other end of the sofa, leaving space between them. The distance felt vast.

"I've been thinking," Margot said. "These past few days. About what you showed me. About what it means."

"Margot, I'm so sorry—"

"Let me finish." Margot held up a hand. "Please. I need to say this, and if you interrupt I don't know if I'll be able to get through it."

Anna nodded. Pressed her lips together. Waited.

Margot took a breath. When she spoke, her voice was careful, controlled—the voice of someone who had rehearsed what they were going to say.

"When I read those letters, I thought—at first—that you were sharing something important to you. Something you loved. And I was touched. I was." She paused. "And then I looked at your face, and I realized what you were actually doing. You were waiting for me to become her. You were hoping I'd read those words and transform into the person who wrote them. Like it was a spell, or a—a manual. Like if I just understood what M. did, I would start doing it too."

Anna's eyes burned. She didn't blink.

"And the thing is," Margot continued, "I've been here before. With other people. Partners who wanted me to be something I wasn't —who had this idea in their head of what a dominant was supposed to look like, supposed to sound like, supposed to be. And they weren't interested in who I actually was. They were interested in whether I could perform their fantasy well enough to make it feel real."

She was looking at Anna now, her eyes bright with something between anger and grief.

"I thought you were different. I thought—when you told me about the letters, about the dynamic you were interested in—I thought we were going to figure it out together. Build something that was ours. Not a recreation of something that belonged to two dead women a century ago."

"I didn't mean—" Anna started.

"But that's exactly what you meant." Margot's voice cracked. "Every time I tried something, every time I gave you a command or held you down or told you what to do—you were grading me. Weren't you? Checking to see if I measured up to her. And I never did. I could see it in your face, even when you told me it was good. There was always this—this *distance*. Like you were waiting for something I wasn't giving you."

Anna couldn't deny it.

"I'm not a fucking Victorian dressmaker, Anna." Margot's voice broke on the words. "I'm a real person. I'm standing right here, trying my best to love you, and you've been having a relationship with a ghost the whole time. I can't compete with that. I can't compete with someone who's been dead for a hundred years and only exists as beautiful words on a page. She never had bad days. She never said the wrong thing. She never failed to give Eleanor exactly what she needed, because the only version of her that exists is the *perfect* version. The edited version. And I'm not edited, Anna. I'm *real.*"

The tears were falling now, down both their faces. Anna couldn't speak. Couldn't find any words that would be enough.

"Do you even know what you want?" Margot asked. "In your own words? Without the letters to borrow from?"

Anna opened her mouth. Closed it. Tried again.

"I—" Her voice came out broken. "I don't know. I've been trying to figure it out. I thought I knew, but—" She shook her head. "The letters gave me words for something I'd felt my whole life but couldn't name. And I thought if I could show you those words, you'd understand. But I never—I never stopped to figure out what *I* wanted. What *my* words were. I just borrowed hers."

"And expected me to live up to them."

"Yes." The admission was agony. "I'm sorry. I'm so sorry. I didn't —I didn't see what I was doing. I thought I was sharing something, but I was—I was setting a test you could never pass. Because you're not her. You were never going to be her. And I kept waiting for you to become someone you couldn't be."

Margot was quiet for a long moment. The tears had stopped, but her face was wet, her mascara smudged. She looked exhausted. Hollowed out.

"I love you," she said quietly. "You know that, right? I've been falling in love with you for months. The real you—the one who notices things, who cares about old objects and old stories, who goes still when I touch her. I love that person."

"But I can't be what you need," Margot continued. "Not if what you need is someone who doesn't exist. Not if you're going to spend the rest of our relationship wishing I was someone else."

"Margot—"

"I need to go." Margot stood up. Her movements were stiff, careful, like she was holding herself together by will alone. "I can't— I can't do this right now. I need to think. I need to figure out if this is something I can get past."

"Please." Anna stood too, reached for her. "Please don't—"

"I'm not saying it's over." Margot stepped back, out of reach. "I'm saying I need time. Real time. Not a few days. I need to know if you can figure out who you are without her words to hide behind. And I need to figure out if I can trust you again. If I can believe that when you look at me, you're seeing me—not measuring me against someone who died before either of us was born."

Anna had nothing to say. No argument, no defence, no way to make this better.

"Goodbye, Anna." Margot walked to the door. Paused with her hand on the handle. "For what it's worth—I hope you find it. What you're looking for. I just don't know if I can be the one to give it to you."

The door opened. The door closed. Footsteps on the stairs, growing fainter.

And then silence.

* * *

Anna stood in the middle of her empty flat and didn't move.

The silence pressed in from all sides. No traffic noise reached this far up. No neighbours moving around. Just her own breathing, and the hum of the refrigerator in the kitchen, and the vast quiet of a space where no one really lived.

She looked around at her white walls, her stacks of books, the laptop still open on the desk with M.'s words on the screen. She closed it. The screen went dark.

Then she sat down on the floor—the sofa felt wrong, too comfortable for this—and wrapped her arms around her knees and let herself fall apart.

Margot was right. About all of it.

Anna walked to the desk and closed the laptop. The screen went dark. M.'s voice, for once, was silent.

She sat down on the floor—she didn't know why, but the sofa felt wrong, too comfortable for what she was feeling—and wrapped her arms around her knees and let herself fall apart.

She cried for a long time. She didn't sort it into categories—Margot, Eleanor, herself. It was all the same grief.

When the tears finally stopped, the flat was dark. Night had fallen while she wasn't paying attention. She sat in the darkness, her back against the wall, her face stiff with dried salt, and thought about what Margot had said.

Do you even know what you want? In your own words?

No. Not yet. But she was going to have to figure it out, and nobody else's language was going to help.

She sat in the dark and started.

CHAPTER 15

A week passed. Then two.

Anna went through the motions. She got up in the morning, showered, dressed, walked to work. She sat at her bench and performed her job—condition assessments, provenance documentation, the careful restoration of objects that had survived longer than any of the people who'd touched them. She ate meals she didn't taste. She slept in fragments, waking at three in the morning to stare at the ceiling and replay every conversation she and Margot had ever had.

She didn't text Margot. Margot didn't text her. The silence was its own kind of answer.

Dr. Fitzwilliam, oblivious to Anna's interior collapse, called her into her office on a grey Tuesday morning.

"The Ashworth proposal," she said, tapping a folder on her desk. "The committee has given preliminary approval. We'll want to move forward with formal cataloguing by April. Can you have the publication draft ready by then?"

"Yes," Anna said. Her voice sounded strange to her own ears—flat, mechanical. "Of course."

"Excellent." Dr. Fitzwilliam peered at her over her reading glasses. "Are you quite all right? You look rather pale."

"I'm fine. Just tired."

"Well, don't overwork yourself. The letters aren't going any-where." A dry smile. "They've waited a hundred and thirty years. They can wait a few more months."

Anna nodded and retreated to her workbench and opened the transcription file she'd been avoiding for days.

She shouldn't look at them. She knew she shouldn't. The letters were the problem—the source of the infection, the poison she'd let seep into everything good. Every time she read M.'s words, she felt herself slipping back into the fantasy, back into the borrowed vocabulary that had cost her Margot.

But Dr. Fitzwilliam had asked for a publication draft. And Anna was nothing if not professional.

She began to read.

* * *

At first, it was the same as always. M.'s measured voice, Eleanor's passionate responses, the careful architecture of their relationship unfolding across page after page. Anna felt the old pull—the seduc-tion of it, the way the words wrapped around her and promised something she'd been craving her whole life.

But Margot's voice was in her head now, asking questions Anna had never thought to ask.

She never had bad days. She never said the wrong thing.

Anna stopped at a letter from March 1888. She'd read it dozens of times—one of her favourites, full of M.'s precise instructions and Eleanor's grateful compliance. But now she noticed something she'd glossed over before: a gap in the dates. The previous letter was from early February. Six weeks of silence, unexplained.

What had happened in those six weeks? A quarrel? A misun-derstanding? Some negotiation that had gone wrong and required mending? The letters didn't say. They picked up again as if nothing had happened, as if the relationship had simply continued in its perfect groove.

But relationships didn't work that way. Not real ones.

Anna scrolled through the transcriptions, looking for other gaps. They were everywhere, once she started noticing them. A month here. Three weeks there. Periods where the letters went thin and formal before suddenly blooming back into intimacy.

What had filled those silences? Arguments? Disappointments? Moments when M. failed to be perfect, when Eleanor failed to be grateful, when the beautiful architecture crumbled and had to be rebuilt?

She'd never wondered before. She'd read the letters as a continuous narrative, smoothing over the gaps, assuming that what wasn't recorded simply hadn't happened. But that wasn't how archives worked. That wasn't how *anything* worked. The gaps were as meaningful as the words. The silences told their own story.

The only version of her that exists is the perfect version, Margot had said. *The edited version.*

Anna stared at her screen and felt the first crack in the thing she'd built. Not quite understanding—not yet—but the beginning of it.

* * *

That weekend, she went to the conservation lab.

The green silk dress had been transferred there two weeks ago, part of the formal cataloguing process. It hung now in a climate-controlled storage room, protected by acid-free tissue and careful temperature management. Anna had the access codes; she could examine it whenever she wanted.

She'd been avoiding it. The dress felt too charged, too connected to everything she'd lost. But the publication would need detailed documentation of the textile evidence, and that meant photographs, measurements, a thorough condition assessment. Professional obligations, again, overriding personal pain.

She let herself into the lab at nine on a Saturday morning, when the building was empty. The dress hung on a padded form, the green silk gleaming dully in the low conservation lighting. It looked smaller than she remembered. More fragile.

Anna pulled on her cotton gloves and began the examination.

She'd studied the dress before, of course—had found the hidden boning, the weighted hem, all the alterations that made it more than just a garment. But that had been discovery, excitement, the thrill of confirmation. Now she looked with different eyes.

She measured the bodice. The proportions weren't standard—thirty-four inches at the bust, twenty-two at the waist, the distance from shoulder to hip slightly longer on the left side than the right. Not sizing for a catalogue. Sizing for a woman. These were Eleanor's measurements. Eleanor's body, encoded in fabric.

The hidden boning along the left seam—Anna ran her fingers over it, feeling its placement through the lining. It pressed at a specific point on the ribcage. Eleanor's ribcage. M. had known exactly where Eleanor was sensitive, exactly where pressure would register, exactly how much constraint would feel like presence rather than pain.

The weights in the hem were distributed unevenly, she noticed now. Heavier on one side than the other. She'd assumed before that this was deliberate—some symbolic significance—but now she wondered if it was simpler than that. Eleanor had walked with a slight imbalance, perhaps. A tendency to favor one leg. M. had compensated, adjusted the weights so the dress would fall correctly on Eleanor's body, with Eleanor's gait.

Every alteration was like that, Anna realized. Specific. Personal. Made for one woman, to be worn by one woman, in the context of one relationship.

This wasn't a template. It wasn't a manual for how dominance and submission should work. It was a garment—a physical object created by one person for another person, shaped by their specific needs, their specific bodies, their specific history together.

The dress was bespoke. The relationship was bespoke. And Anna had been trying to wear both of them as if they were off-the-rack.

She stood in the empty lab, her gloved hands resting on the green silk, and finally understood what Margot had been trying to tell her.

She couldn't borrow M.'s voice because M.'s voice had been shaped for Eleanor. The commands, the rituals, the precise architecture of their dynamic—all of it had been built through negotiation, through trial and error, through the messy process of two people figuring out how to fit together. The letters were the highlight reel, but underneath them was a foundation of conversations that hadn't been recorded. Arguments that hadn't been preserved. Failures and adjustments and compromises that had been smoothed away by time and selective archiving.

M. hadn't known instinctively what Eleanor needed. She'd learned it. The same way Margot had been trying to learn what Anna needed—through attention, through experimentation, through the slow accumulation of knowledge that only came from being present with another person.

Anna pressed her forehead against the cool fabric of the dress form and closed her eyes.

"I'm sorry," she said to the empty room, and meant it for everyone.

* * *

She sat with the dress for a long time.

The light through the high windows shifted from morning grey to pale afternoon gold. Anna didn't move. She was thinking—really thinking, for the first time—about what she wanted. Not what M. had wanted for Eleanor. Not what the letters made her feel. What *she*, Anna, actually wanted.

She wanted structure. That much was real—her own, not borrowed. She wanted the relief of not having to decide, of having someone else hold the shape of things while she existed inside it.

But the specific shape? The commands, the exact rituals, the precise architecture? Those couldn't be inherited. Those had to be built. With another person. Through conversation and failure and the slow, awkward process of two people learning each other's edges.

Margot had been willing to do that work. Had been doing it, for months, adjusting and experimenting and trying to find the configuration that fit. And Anna had been grading her performance against a standard Margot had never agreed to, judging her failures against a blueprint she'd never been shown.

God, she'd been unfair. So catastrophically, selfishly unfair.

The question wasn't whether she could have what Eleanor and M. had. She couldn't—that relationship was gone, specific to two people in a specific time and place, unrepeatable. The question was whether she could build something of her own. Something that fit her body, her life, her shape.

And the harder question: whether Margot would still be willing to build it with her.

Anna stood up. Her legs were stiff from sitting so long. She looked at the dress one more time—the green silk, the hidden alterations, the material evidence of a love story that had ended a hundred and thirty years ago.

"Thank you," she said quietly. Not to the dress, exactly. To Eleanor and M., maybe. To the parts of herself that had needed to learn this lesson. "I think I understand now."

She covered the dress carefully with its protective tissue, turned off the lights, and locked the lab behind her.

Outside, the February afternoon was cold and bright. Anna stood on the steps of the building and breathed in the sharp air and thought about what she was going to say.

She was going to have to find her own words. That was the thing. After all this time hiding behind M.'s elegant prose, she was going to have to speak in her own voice—clumsy, imperfect, nothing like the letters. She was going to have to tell Margot what she wanted, not by pointing to someone else's relationship but by articulating her own needs, however badly.

It was terrifying. It was the only thing that might work.

Anna pulled out her phone, hesitated, put it away. Not yet. She needed to figure out what she was going to say first. Needed to find the words—her own words, not borrowed ones—for everything she should have said months ago.

She walked home through the cold bright streets, and for the first time in weeks, she didn't think about the letters at all.

CHAPTER 16

She wrote the text seventeen times before she sent it.

The first attempts were too long—paragraphs of explanation, apology, self-justification. She deleted them all. Margot didn't need her excuses. Margot needed to know that Anna had heard her, had understood, had changed. And that couldn't be communicated in a wall of text.

The later attempts were too short—*Can we talk?* or *I'm sorry* or *I miss you.* All true, but not enough. Not the words Margot deserved.

In the end, she settled on something in between:

I've been thinking about what you said. You were right—about all of it. I've been trying to figure out my own words, not borrowed ones. I don't know if I've found them yet, but I'd like to try to explain. If you're willing to listen. No pressure. I understand if you're not.

She stared at the message for ten minutes. Then she pressed send before she could talk herself out of it.

The response came three hours later, while Anna was pretending to read a journal article about eighteenth-century bookbinding techniques.

Coffee tomorrow? The place on Little Clarendon. 2pm.

Not Margot's flat. Not Anna's. Neutral ground.

I'll be there, Anna typed back.

She didn't sleep that night.

* * *

The café was busy with the Sunday afternoon crowd—students with laptops, couples sharing cake, a group of elderly women having an animated discussion about someone named Patricia. Anna arrived fifteen minutes early and claimed a table in the corner, away from the noise.

She ordered a coffee she didn't want and sat with her hands wrapped around the cup, watching the door.

Margot arrived exactly on time. She was wearing her grey coat, the one she'd been wearing the night they met for coffee all those months ago. Anna didn't know if that was deliberate or coincidence. She didn't know anything anymore.

Margot spotted her, crossed the room, sat down across from her. She didn't smile. Didn't reach for Anna's hand. Just settled into her chair and looked at her with an expression Anna couldn't read.

"Hi," Anna said.

"Hi."

A server appeared. Margot ordered a tea without looking at the menu. When they were alone again, she said, "You wanted to explain."

No small talk. No easing into it. Anna appreciated that, in a painful way.

"I went to see the dress," she said. "Last weekend. I was supposed to be documenting it for the publication, but I—" She stopped. Started again. "I finally understood something. About why I was so wrong."

Margot waited. Her face gave nothing away.

"The dress was made for Eleanor. Specifically for her—her measurements, her body, her relationship with M. The alterations fit her. They wouldn't fit anyone else. They weren't meant to." Anna took a breath. "And I've been trying to wear it anyway. Trying to make you fit into something that was designed for someone else. Someone who lived a hundred and thirty years ago, in a completely different world, with completely different needs."

"The letters too," Margot said quietly. "You were trying to make us fit those."

"Yes. And I didn't even see the letters properly until you—until after." Anna forced herself to meet Margot's eyes. "I went back and read them again. Really read them. And I noticed all the gaps. All the silences. The weeks where nothing was recorded, the periods where something clearly went wrong and had to be repaired. The letters aren't the whole relationship. They're just the highlights. The parts that were beautiful enough to keep."

"The edited version," Margot said. There was no triumph in her voice. Just tiredness.

"The edited version." Anna nodded. "You were right. I was comparing you to something that never existed. Not really. M. and Eleanor had bad days too—they must have. They argued, they disappointed each other, they probably had nights when the whole thing felt impossible. But none of that survived. Just the good parts. Just the poetry."

Margot's tea arrived. She wrapped her hands around the cup but didn't drink.

"Why are you telling me this?" she asked. "What do you want, Anna?"

The question Anna had been dreading. The one she had to answer in her own words.

"I want—" Her voice caught. She made herself continue. "I want to try again. With you. But differently. Not trying to recreate

something that belonged to other people. Actually building something. Together."

"And what would that look like?"

"I don't know." It was terrifying to admit. "I know I want
—structure. I know I want someone to hold the shape of things sometimes, so I don't have to. But the specific shape? What that actually
looks like in practice? I don't know. I've never done this before. Not
really. I just borrowed someone else's blueprint and pretended it was
mine."

Margot was quiet for a long moment. The café noise washed
around them—laughter from the students, the hiss of the espresso
machine, Patricia's continued misadventures. Anna waited.

"Can I tell you something?" Margot said finally.

"Please."

"The woman I told you about—the one who taught me. She
warned me about this, actually. People who fall in love with a particular version of the dynamic—something they read about, or imagined,
or saw somewhere—and they get so attached to that version that they
can't see the actual person trying to do it with them." Margot's voice
was careful, measured.

"That's exactly what I did."

"Yes." Margot finally took a sip of her tea. "And I knew it was
happening. I could feel it. Every time we were together, I could sense
you—waiting. Measuring. Checking to see if I was doing it right. And
I kept trying to figure out what 'right' meant, but I couldn't, because
the rules were in your head and you wouldn't share them."

"I'm sorry." The words felt inadequate. "I'm so sorry."

"I know you are." Margot set down her cup. "And I believe
you've changed. Or started to. I can hear it in the way you're talking
—you're actually thinking about this, not just reciting someone else's
ideas."

"But?"

"But I need to tell you something too. About what I want. Because you asked me to be honest, and I wasn't—not completely. I was so focused on trying to give you what you needed that I never really said what I needed."

Anna's heart clenched. "Tell me."

Margot was quiet for a moment, gathering her thoughts.

"I like control," she said finally. "I do. I like being in charge, giving direction, having someone trust me enough to follow. But it's not—" She paused, searching for words. "It's not a religion for me. It's not an identity. It's something I do sometimes, with someone I care about, because it's fun and it's hot and it makes us both feel good. But I don't want to be someone's whole world. I don't want to be responsible for someone else's sense of self."

Anna nodded slowly. She was starting to understand.

"The way M. writes to Eleanor—it's beautiful, but it's *heavy*," Margot continued. "She's Eleanor's whole framework. Everything Eleanor understands about herself comes through M. And maybe that worked for them, in their time, with their circumstances. But I can't be that for someone. I don't want to be. I want a partner, not a —a disciple."

"I don't want you to be my whole framework," Anna said. "I thought I did, but—that's part of what I realized. I was looking for someone to tell me who I was. To give me an identity, a shape, a way of understanding myself. And that's not fair. That's not what a relationship is supposed to be."

"No," Margot agreed. "It's not."

"I need to figure out who I am on my own. What I want, in my own words. And then—if there's still something between us—we can build something together. Something that fits both of us. Not a recreation of M. and Eleanor. Something new."

Margot studied her across the table. The wariness was still there, but something else too—something that might have been hope, maybe?

"That sounds healthy," she said slowly. "In theory. But how do I know you're not just saying what I want to hear? How do I know that the first time I don't meet some expectation you haven't told me about, we won't be right back here?"

"You don't." Anna's voice was steady, even though her heart was pounding. "I can't promise I won't make mistakes. I can't promise I've figured everything out. But I can promise to try. To tell you when something isn't working instead of waiting for you to read my mind. To use my own words even when they're clumsy and imperfect and nothing like the letters."

"That's a lot of promises."

"I know. And you don't have to believe any of them. You don't have to give me another chance. I'd understand if—" Anna's voice wavered. "I'd understand if you didn't want to try again. After everything I put you through. But I had to at least tell you. That I see it now. What I did. What I should have done differently."

Margot was quiet for a long time. Around them, the café continued its Sunday afternoon rhythms—cups clinking, conversations flowing, life going on as usual while Anna's future hung in the balance.

"I've missed you," Margot said finally. "These past weeks. Even angry, even hurt—I've missed you."

"I've missed you too." Anna's eyes were burning. "So much."

"I'm not saying yes." Margot held up a hand. "I'm not saying we're back together, or that everything's fine, or that I trust you again. But I'm—" She took a breath. "I'm willing to try. Slowly. Carefully. With a lot of talking and a lot of checking in and absolutely no more Victorian letters used as relationship guides."

Anna laughed—a wet, broken sound. "No more Victorian letters. I promise."

"I mean it." But Margot was almost smiling now. "If you ever hand me a historical document and expect me to divine your desires from it, I'm walking out and not coming back."

"Fair." Anna wiped her eyes. "Completely fair."

They sat in silence for a moment. Not the heavy silence of before—something lighter. Something that felt like a beginning, fragile and uncertain and tentatively hopeful.

"So," Margot said. "What now?"

"I don't know." Anna found that she was smiling, despite everything. "I've never done this part before either."

"Well." Margot picked up her tea again. "I suppose we'll figure it out. Together. One awkward conversation at a time."

"I'd like that," Anna said. "I'd really like that."

Outside the café windows, the February afternoon was fading into evening. Inside, their tea and coffee had gone cold. Neither of them moved to leave.

CHAPTER 17

They started over. Slowly. Carefully. Like two people learning a new language together.

Coffee dates first—public places, neutral ground, conversations that circled around what they'd been and what they might become. They talked about their days, their work, the small ordinary things that made up a life. They didn't talk about the letters. They didn't talk about what had gone wrong. Not yet. They were building a foundation first, brick by careful brick.

Two weeks in, Margot invited Anna to her flat for dinner. "My turn to sit and watch," she said. "You cook. I'll try not to backseat drive."

Anna laughed—a real laugh, surprised out of her. "You're going to hate that."

"Probably. But I want to see you in a kitchen. I want to know what you're like when you're in charge of something."

The words landed strangely. Anna had never thought of herself as in charge of anything. But she agreed, and spent two days planning a menu she could actually execute, and showed up at Margot's flat on Saturday afternoon with bags of groceries.

Margot's kitchen felt different when Anna was the one standing at the stove. Smaller, somehow. More intimidating. Every surface seemed designed for someone who knew what they were doing.

"You're hovering," Anna said, without turning around.

"I'm observing." Margot was perched on the stool at the counter—Anna's usual spot—with a glass of wine. "There's a difference."

"You're hovering and it's making me nervous."

"Okay, fair." Margot made a visible effort to relax. "What are you making?"

"Risotto." Anna stirred the rice, watching it absorb the wine. "It's the only thing I'm actually good at. My grandmother taught me when I was twelve. She said it teaches you patience."

"Does it?"

"I don't know. I'm not particularly patient." Anna added another ladle of stock. "But I can make risotto, so something stuck."

She could feel Margot watching her. Not critically—she didn't think—just attentively. The same focused attention Margot brought to everything.

"You're different in here," Margot said after a while. "More—I don't know. Present. You're not in your head so much."

"The risotto requires attention. If I think about other things, I'll ruin it."

"Is that why you like it?"

Anna considered. "Maybe. It's—there's a structure. You have to do things in a certain order, at a certain pace. You can't rush it or skip steps. And if you follow the structure, it works." She glanced back at Margot. "I suppose that's a theme for me."

"Structure."

"Structure." Anna turned back to the stove. "I like knowing the rules. I like having a framework. It's—calming. When I know what

I'm supposed to do, I can actually do it. It's the not knowing that paralyzes me."

"Is that what you want from—" Margot paused. "From us? When we're—together?"

They hadn't talked about this directly since the café. They'd been circling it, both of them, waiting for the right moment.

"Yes," she said. "I think so. I want—" She stopped, frustrated. "This is the part where I don't have words."

"Try anyway."

Anna kept stirring. It was easier to talk when she didn't have to make eye contact.

"I want to not have to decide," she said slowly. "Sometimes. Not all the time—I'm not looking for someone to run my whole life. But in—in bed. I want someone else to hold the structure. To tell me what to do so I don't have to figure it out myself. So I can just—be. Without all the noise in my head about whether I'm doing it right, whether I'm being good enough, whether—" She broke off. "Does that make sense?"

"Yes," Margot said quietly. "It makes sense."

"And I know that's—I know I was unfair before. Expecting you to read my mind, to somehow know the shape of what I wanted without me telling you. I know I need to be clearer. I just—" Anna added more stock, watching it absorb. "I don't always have the words in the moment. When I'm turned on, when things are happening, my brain doesn't work the way it does now. I can't articulate things. I can only respond."

"So we talk about it beforehand." Margot's voice was thoughtful. "Like this. When you can think clearly. And then, in the moment, I can—work within whatever framework we've agreed on."

"Yes." Anna felt something loosen in her chest. "Yes, exactly. Is that—can you work with that?"

"I can work with that." Margot was quiet for a moment. "But I need you to understand something too. I'm not going to be—" She paused, searching for words. "Formal. Scripted. Whatever you were imagining from those letters. That's not me. If I'm going to tell you what to do, it's going to sound like me. It might be playful, or teasing, or—I don't know. Whatever feels right in the moment. Not composed. Not elegant."

"I don't need elegant," Anna said. "I thought I did. But I don't. I just need—" She turned around, finally meeting Margot's eyes. "I just need you to mean it. Whatever you say. I need to know it's real, not performance."

"I can do real," Margot said. A small smile tugged at the corner of her mouth. "Real is kind of my specialty."

Anna smiled back. It felt strange on her face—unfamiliar after weeks of tension and grief. But good. Real.

"Your risotto's going to burn," Margot said.

"Shit—" Anna spun back to the stove, stirring frantically. The rice was fine. Margot was laughing.

"Gotcha," she said. "Couldn't resist."

"You're terrible."

"I am. You like it."

Anna found that she did.

* * *

The risotto was good. Not as good as Margot's cooking, but good —creamy and rich, the parmesan melted through, the mushrooms earthy and deep. They ate at the counter, side by side, their shoulders almost touching.

"Your grandmother taught you well," Margot said, scraping her bowl.

"She'd be horrified by my knife skills. But she'd approve of the taste."

"Your knife skills are fine."

"You were biting your tongue the entire time I was chopping."

"I was not." A pause. "I was biting it a little. You hold the knife wrong."

"I know." Anna bumped her shoulder against Margot's. "Thank you for not saying anything."

"It was painful. But I managed."

They sat in comfortable silence for a moment. The flat was warm, the wine was good, and for the first time in weeks Anna felt something like peace.

"Can I ask you something?" Margot said.

"Yes."

"Are we—" Margot turned to face her. "I mean, tonight. Are we just having dinner? Or is this—" She gestured vaguely between them.

"I don't know," Anna admitted. "What do you want it to be?"

"I asked you first."—

Anna took a breath. This was the part where she had to use her words. Her own words.

"I want—" She stopped. Started again. "I've missed you. Not just the—the sex. All of it. Being with you. Talking to you. Waking up next to you. And I know we're supposed to be going slow. And I don't want to rush anything. But if you wanted to—if you were ready —I would like. Tonight. To be more than dinner."

Margot was quiet for a long moment. Then she reached out and took Anna's hand.

"I've missed you too," she said. "And I think—I think I'm ready to try. If we can do it differently this time. If we can talk to each other instead of guessing."

"We can talk," Anna said. "I can try, at least. To tell you what's working. What isn't."

"And if I ask you a question, you'll answer it? Even in the moment? You won't just—" Margot hesitated. "You won't just wish I already knew?"

"I'll try," Anna said honestly. "I can't promise I'll be good at it. But I'll try."

"That's all I'm asking." Margot squeezed her hand. "Come on. Leave the dishes. They'll keep."

She stood, still holding Anna's hand, and led her toward the bedroom.

They undressed each other slowly. No rush, no urgency—just the quiet intimacy of buttons and zippers, of fabric falling away, of skin revealed inch by inch.

Anna had forgotten how beautiful Margot was. Or not forgotten, exactly, but the memory had faded, gone thin with absence. Now, standing in the soft lamplight, she saw her again: the strength of her shoulders, the curve of her hips, the confidence in the way she held herself.

"You're staring," Margot said.

"I'm looking." Anna reached out, touched Margot's collarbone. "I forgot how much I like looking at you."

"Yeah?" Margot stepped closer, into Anna's space. "What else did you forget?"

"I don't know yet." Anna's voice came out rougher than she intended. "Remind me."

Margot smiled—not the polished smile from before, not the one she wore when she was trying to be what Anna wanted. This was something realer, warmer. A little crooked.

"Get on the bed," she said. "On your back."

Anna's breath caught. Not at the words themselves—they were simple enough—but at the way Margot said them. Casual. Easy. Like it was the most natural thing in the world to tell Anna what to do.

She climbed onto the bed. Lay back against the pillows. Watched Margot watching her.

"Good," Margot said. She didn't move to join her yet. Just stood at the foot of the bed, looking. "I'm going to touch you now. And I want you to tell me what feels good. Not what you think I want to hear. What actually feels good. Can you do that?"

"I can try."

"Try hard." Margot climbed onto the bed, settled beside her. "I'm serious, Anna. No performing. No pretending. If something doesn't work, you tell me. If something's amazing, you tell me that too. I need actual information, not—" She waved a hand. "Not whatever you think I want."

"Okay." Anna swallowed. "Okay. Yes."

"Good." Margot leaned down and kissed her.

The kiss was slow, thorough. Margot's hand came up to cup Anna's jaw, tilting her head to the angle she wanted. It wasn't a question. It was an adjustment—small, sure, confident. Anna felt herself melt into it, felt her body go soft against the mattress.

Margot broke the kiss. "That. What you just did."

"What?"

"You relaxed. The second I moved your head, you went—" Margot made a gesture. "Soft. Like you'd been holding something tight and suddenly you didn't have to."

"Oh." Anna hadn't noticed. But now that Margot said it, she could feel it—the difference between before and after. The small release. "I like when you—position me. Decide how I should be."

"Noted." Margot kissed her again, then pulled back. "Turn over. On your stomach."

Anna turned. Pressed her face into the pillow, suddenly very aware of her own nakedness. She couldn't see Margot now—could only feel the mattress shift as Margot moved, only hear her breathing.

"I'm going to touch your back," Margot said. "Tell me what you feel."

Her hands landed on Anna's shoulders, warm and firm. Started working down her spine, pressing into the muscles, finding the knots of tension Anna hadn't known she was carrying.

"Good," Anna managed. "That's—yes."

"More specific."

"I—" Anna tried to find words through the fog of sensation. "The pressure. I like the pressure. And not being able to see you. I don't have to—perform an expression. I can just feel."

"Good." Margot's hands moved lower, working the muscles along Anna's spine. "What else?"

"I like that you're telling me to talk. It's—" Anna laughed shakily. "It's paradoxical, I know. But having to answer makes me focus. It keeps me here instead of in my head."

"Interesting." Margot's hands reached the small of Anna's back, pressed in. "So the questions help. Good to know."

She kept going—down Anna's back, over her hips, along her thighs. It wasn't quite a massage, it wasn't quite foreplay. Somewhere in between. Anna felt herself dissolving under the touch, her thoughts going quiet, her body coming alive.

"Turn back over," Margot said eventually. "I want to see your face."

Anna turned. Margot was looking down at her with dark eyes, her expression intent, focused. Not performing—just present.

"Hi," Anna said, suddenly shy.

"Hi yourself." Margot settled over her, one knee between Anna's thighs. "I'm going to touch you now. Really touch you. And you're going to keep talking to me. Tell me what works. What doesn't. What you want more of."

"Okay."

"And Anna?" Margot's hand slid down her stomach, paused just above where Anna wanted it. "Don't come until I tell you to."

The words shot through her like electricity. Just Margot, looking at her with steady eyes, telling her what to do.

"Yes," Anna breathed. "Okay. Yes."

Margot's hand moved lower.

* * *

It was different this time. Messier. More awkward. Anna stumbled over her words, couldn't always articulate what she was feeling, sometimes said things that made no sense at all. Margot asked questions—*here? like this? harder?*—and Anna answered as best she could, and sometimes the answers were wrong and they had to adjust.

But underneath the awkwardness, something was working. Anna could feel it—the structure taking shape, the dynamic building not from a blueprint but from the actual moment. Margot's voice in her ear, steady and certain. Margot's hands on her body, learning her responses in real time. The command—*don't come until I tell you*—holding her in place, giving her something to push against.

She got close. Closer. Her hips were moving despite herself, her breath coming in gasps, her whole body straining toward release.

"Not yet," Margot murmured, and Anna whimpered but obeyed, pulling back from the edge.

"Please—"

"Tell me what you need."

"I need—" Anna's mind was blank, white, nothing but sensation. "I need you to tell me. When. I need—please—"

"You need me to decide."

"Yes." It came out broken, desperate. "Yes, please, I can't—I need you to—"

Margot leaned down, her lips brushing Anna's ear.

"Come for me," she said. "Now. Let go."

Anna let go.

The orgasm hit her like a wall, left her shaking and gasping and clutching at Margot's shoulders like she might drown without something to hold onto. Margot stayed with her through it, murmuring things Anna couldn't parse, her hand still moving, drawing out every last tremor until Anna was wrung out and boneless.

"There you go," Margot said softly. "That's it. I've got you."

Anna opened her eyes. Margot was looking down at her, flushed and breathing hard herself, but her gaze was warm, present. Not performing. Not checking to see if she'd done it right.

Just there. With her.

"Hi," Anna said again, stupid with endorphins.

"Hi." Margot laughed and kissed her forehead. "Was that—did that work?"

"Yes." Anna pulled her down, wrapped her arms around her. "Yes. That was—yes."

"Eloquent."

"Shut up. My brain isn't working." Anna buried her face in Margot's shoulder. "Give me a minute and I'll—I want to—you haven't—"

"We have time." Margot's arms tightened around her. "We have all the time we need. No rush."

They lay tangled together, breathing. Anna's heart rate slowly returned to normal. She was thinking about what had just happened —the way Margot had asked questions, the way she'd had to answer.

It hadn't been like the letters. It hadn't been elegant or composed or anything like what she'd imagined. But it had been real. It had been *Margot*—playful and direct and impossibly herself. An expression of dominance, not a performance of it. It wasn't borrowed from anyone else. It was simply hers.

And Anna had responded. Not to a ghost, not to a fantasy, but to the actual woman in front of her.

"Margot?"

"Mm?"

"Thank you. For—asking. For making me talk. I know it's not —" Anna struggled to find the words. "I know it doesn't match what I said I wanted. The whole point was supposed to be not having to think. And you made me think the whole time."

"Did it work anyway?"

Anna considered. "Yes. Different than I expected. But yes. The questions—they kept me present. I couldn't drift off into fantasy. I had to stay here, with you. And that was—" She paused. "That was better. Actually."

"Good." Margot pressed a kiss to her hair. "That's what I was hoping. That we could find a way to make it work for both of us. You get the structure. I get to check in. We both stay present."

"Is that what you want?" Anna pulled back to look at her. "I never asked. What you actually want. What makes it good for you."

"I like watching you let go," Margot said simply. "I like being the one who gets you there.

Anna filed that away. Information about what Margot liked. A piece of the architecture they were building together.

"Your turn," she said, rolling them over so Margot was beneath her. "Tell me what you want."

Margot grinned up at her. "Now you're getting it."

* * *

Later—much later, after they'd explored and talked and laughed at their own awkwardness and made each other come in ways that were entirely their own—they lay in the dark, limbs intertwined.

"This is going to take practice," Margot said sleepily. "The talking thing. We're not going to get it right every time."

"I know."

"And I'm going to ask you questions you don't know how to answer. And sometimes you're going to want something you can't articulate and you'll get frustrated and I'll get frustrated and it'll be a mess."

"I know." Anna traced a pattern on Margot's shoulder. "But we'll figure it out. Keep adjusting. Keep building."

"Like the risotto."

Anna laughed. "Like the risotto. One step at a time. Patient."

"You said you weren't patient."

"I'm learning." Anna pressed a kiss to Margot's shoulder. "I'm learning a lot of things."

Margot pulled her closer, and they fell asleep like that—holding each other in the dark, beginning to figure out who they could be together.

It was enough. It was more than enough.

It was theirs.

CHAPTER 18

Spring came to Oxford in shades of green and gold—crocuses pushing through the college lawns, wisteria beginning to climb the old stone walls, tourists returning in force to photograph the dreaming spires. The days lengthened, the light softened, and Anna found herself noticing things she hadn't noticed in months. The quality of morning sun through her office window. The smell of cut grass drifting up from the quad. The way the city seemed to shake itself awake after the long grey winter.

She was happy. The word still surprised her sometimes—caught her off guard in ordinary moments, making her pause mid-task to examine the unfamiliar feeling. Happy. Was that what this was? This steady warmth, this sense of rightness, this absence of the constant reaching for something she couldn't name?

It had been three months since the night she'd made risotto in Margot's kitchen. Three months of building something together—awkward conversations and better sex and the slow accumulation of shared knowledge that was, she was learning, what a relationship actually looked like. Not a finished structure but an ongoing construction. Always adjusting. Always learning.

They'd found rhythms that worked. Margot gave directions in bed—casual, playful, unmistakably hers—and Anna followed them, and talked when Margot asked her to talk, and was learning to articulate things she'd never had words for before. It wasn't perfect. Some nights the communication misfired, or Anna got stuck in her head, or Margot's style didn't quite land. But they talked about it afterward. Adjusted. Tried again.

"Progress, not perfection," Margot had said once, quoting something from a self-help book she'd been reading. Anna had rolled her eyes, but she'd also written it down later. It felt like something worth remembering.

* * *

On a Thursday morning in early April, Anna received an email from Dr. Fitzwilliam.

The committee has given final approval for the Ashworth collection. Full cataloguing to proceed immediately. Publication timeline confirmed for autumn. Please prepare the materials for archival processing.

Anna read it twice, waiting for the rush of triumph she'd expected. It came, but muted—satisfaction rather than elation. The letters would be preserved. The dress would be documented. The story of Eleanor and M. would be available for other researchers, other curious minds, other people who might find in those pages something they recognized.

It was what she'd wanted. It was good work, important work. But it no longer felt like the centre of her life.

She replied to Dr. Fitzwilliam, confirming she would begin archival processing the following week. Then she texted Margot.

Proposal approved. Letters and dress officially part of the university collection now.

The response came a few minutes later: *That's wonderful! Congratulations. Dinner tonight to celebrate?*

Yes please. Your place?

Obviously. I'll cook something special. See you at 7.

Anna smiled at her phone, set it aside, and went back to work.

* * *

The conservation lab was quiet on Saturday afternoon. Anna had come in alone, wanting privacy for this—the final handling of the dress before it went into permanent archival storage.

The green silk hung on its padded form, the same as it had for months now. But today felt different. Final. After this, the dress would be wrapped in acid-free tissue, sealed in a climate-controlled box, filed away in the depths of the textile repository. Available for research, but no longer hers to touch whenever she wanted.

She pulled on her cotton gloves and approached the form.

The fabric was cool under her fingers, even through the gloves. Faded now from the forest green it must have been, but still beautiful —the drape of the silk, the precision of the seams, the invisible architecture M. had built into every fold. Anna traced the left side seam, feeling the hidden boning beneath the lining. She knew this dress now. Knew it better, probably, than anyone alive.

She thought about Eleanor, standing in M.'s workshop all those years ago, being fitted for this garment. Had she known, that first time, what she was agreeing to? Had she understood what it would mean to wear M.'s work against her skin, to carry their secret into rooms full of people who couldn't see it?

Probably not. Nobody understood at the beginning. You had to live it first—had to feel the shape of your own wanting—before you could recognize what you'd found.

The dress fit Eleanor because it had been made for Eleanor— every seam, every alteration, every hidden constraint shaped for her particular form.

Anna's form was different. Her life was different. Her relation-ship with Margot was nothing like what Eleanor and M. had built —messier, less elegant, full of stumbles and miscommunications and awkward conversations at two in the morning when something hadn't worked and they were both too tired to be graceful about it.

She let her hand rest on the bodice for a moment, feeling the structure beneath the silk. Then she stepped back.

"Thank you," she said to the empty room. "For showing me what was possible."

She stepped back. Looked at the dress one last time—the green silk gleaming softly in the conservation lighting, the careful construction that had survived more than a century.

Then she began the work of wrapping it for storage.

* * *

The process was methodical, familiar. Lay out the acid-free tissue. Support the bodice, the sleeves, the skirt. Fold carefully to avoid stress on the seams. Layer more tissue. Ease into the archival box, checking at every stage for proper positioning.

Anna had done this hundreds of times with other garments. But this one she handled more slowly, more deliberately. Not because it was fragile—though it was—but because she wanted to remember. The weight of the silk in her hands. The faint smell of age and preservation. The texture of fabric that had been worn and loved and kept.

The letters were already processed, catalogued and filed in the archives. She'd done that work last week—scanning each page, creating detailed records, building the documentation that would let future researchers understand what they were looking at. Someone, someday, would find them and wonder. Would read M.'s words and feel something shift in their chest. Would recognize, as Anna had recognized, a shape they didn't have a name for.

She hoped whoever it was would be braver than she'd been. Would use the letters as a starting point, not a destination. Would find their own words, their own shape, their own way of wanting.

The dress settled into its box. Anna arranged the final layers of tissue, checked the placement one more time, and lifted the lid.

She paused with the lid in her hands, looking down at the wrapped bundle of green silk.

Goodbye, she thought. And thank you. For everything.

She closed the lid and sealed the box.

The evening light was golden when Anna left the conservation building, the April sun hanging low over the spires and rooftops. She walked through the familiar streets with the archival box tucked under her arm—she'd drop it at the textile repository on Monday, but for now it was hers to carry.

Her phone buzzed. Margot.

Lamb is in the oven. Wine is breathing. Where are you?

On my way. Ten minutes.

Good. Don't be late.

Anna smiled. A year ago, she would have read those words and heard M.'s voice underneath—would have searched for hidden meaning, for the echo of Victorian command. Now she just heard Margot. Teasing. Warm. Real.

She walked faster.

* * *

Margot's flat was warm with the smell of roasting lamb and rosemary. Anna let herself in—she had a key now, had had one for two months, still felt a small thrill every time she used it—and found Margot in the kitchen, wiping her hands on a towel.

"There you are." Margot crossed the room and kissed her. "How was it? The dress?"

"Good. Sad. Done." Anna set the archival box on the counter. "It's ready for storage now. I'll take it to the repository on Monday."

"Are you okay?"

Anna considered the question. "Yes," she said, and meant it. "It's strange, letting go of something I've been living with for so long. But it's—it's time. It belongs to the archive now. Not to me."

Margot nodded. She didn't say anything else—didn't push for more, didn't try to fix the complicated feelings Anna was still sorting through. Just accepted it, as she'd learned to accept so much about Anna.

"Wine?" she asked.

"Please."

Margot poured her a glass, and they moved to the sofa—their usual positions now, familiar as breathing. Anna tucked herself into the corner, and Margot settled beside her, close enough that their shoulders touched.

"So," Margot said. "Now that you've said goodbye to the Victorian lesbians. What's next?"

Anna laughed. "I don't know. More conservation work. More cataloguing. Dr. Fitzwilliam mentioned a collection of eighteenth-century trade cards that needs assessment."

"Trade cards. Thrilling."

"Shut up. They're historically significant."

"I'm sure they are." Margot's eyes were warm with amusement. "Any secret love affairs hidden among them?"

"Probably not. But you never know what you'll find." Anna took a sip of wine. "That's the thing about archives. They're full of surprises."

"So are people."

"So are people," Anna agreed.

They sat in comfortable silence for a moment. The evening light slanted through the windows, turning the room gold. Somewhere in the kitchen, a timer beeped.

"That's the lamb," Margot said, but she didn't move. "Give me one more minute."

"Okay."

Margot turned to look at her. Her expression was soft, unguarded—the face she wore only in private, only with Anna.

"I'm proud of you," she said. "For all of it. The publication, the catalogue, the—" She gestured vaguely. "The letting go."

"I couldn't have done it without you."

"You could have. You would have figured it out eventually. But I'm glad I got to be here for it."

Anna leaned over and kissed her—soft, unhurried, full of things she was still learning how to say.

"Me too," she said. "I'm glad you're here."

The timer beeped again, more insistently.

"Okay, okay." Margot stood, pulled Anna up with her. "Come on. Help me with the plates. And then you can tell me everything about Eleanor and M. that didn't make it into the official catalogue."

"The scandalous bits?"

"Obviously the scandalous bits. What's the point of dating an archivist if I don't get the classified information?"

Anna laughed and followed her into the kitchen, and they made dinner together the way they'd learned to do everything together—imperfectly, with a lot of talking, adjusting as they went.

Later that night, lying in Margot's bed with the window cracked open to the spring air, Anna thought about the dress in its box. Wrapped in tissue. Waiting to be filed away. Eleanor and M.'s story, preserved and documented and ready for someone else to find.

Margot shifted in her sleep, throwing an arm across Anna's stomach. Warm. Heavy. Real.

Anna closed her eyes.

Tomorrow there would be more work—more cataloguing, more conversations, more of the slow patient labour of two people figuring each other out. But tonight she was here, in a bed that smelled like rosemary and wine, and she didn't want to be anywhere else.

APPENDIX

The Ashworth Correspondence

The following letters were discovered in 2019 as part of the Ashworth family bequest to the Bodleian Library. They document the relationship between Eleanor Mary Ashworth (1857-1943) and her dressmaker, known only as M., between November 1887 and September 1889. The correspondence has been transcribed in full and is reproduced here with permission.

I.

Thursday 3rd November 1887

My dearest—

I have thought of nothing but Thursday since you left me. You must know this. You must feel it too, this thread that stretches between us even now, even as I write these words knowing you will not read them for days. I am yours across any distance. I am yours in the spaces between heartbeats.

You told me to be patient. I am trying. But patience is a discipline I have not yet mastered, not in this. Not when I can still feel where your hands rested at my waist. Not when I close my eyes and see you looking at me as you did when you dismissed me. That look. I have no words for that look except to say that I understood, in that moment, what it would mean to belong to someone entirely.

I have never belonged to anyone. I did not know I wanted to.

You have made me know.

Thursday cannot come soon enough.

Yours—entirely, always—

E.

II.

Thursday 10th November 1887

You ask if I think of you. You ask as though there were doubt. I wonder sometimes if you understand what you are, what you have already become to me. I suspect you do not. You came to me for a dress and did not know you were offering something else entirely.

I think of little else.

But thinking is not the same as speaking, and I have never been skilled at speaking. My hands know things my words cannot manage. What I can do is show you. What I can do is wait for Thursday, and know that you will come to me, and trust that when you stand before me you will understand everything I cannot write.

Be patient. I am teaching you something. You do not yet know what it is.

Yours—

M.

III.

Monday 14th November 1887

I came home from you today and sat in my room for an hour without moving. Not because I was tired, though I was tired. Not because I was thinking, though I was thinking. Because you had not told me I could move, and some part of me was still waiting for permission.

Is that madness? It feels like madness. It feels like the sanest thing I have ever done.

You say I do not understand what I am becoming. You are right. I do not. I only know that before I met you I moved through the world like a guest in my own body, and now—now I am beginning to feel that I live there. That someone has given me the key.

Thursday was not enough. It is never enough. I stand in your workshop and time stops and then I leave and it begins again and everything between our Thursdays is just waiting. I am made of waiting, now. You have made me so.

Tell me what you want of me. Tell me and I will do it. I will do anything.

Yours—always, entirely—

E.

IV.

Thursday 17th November 1887

You ask me to tell you what I want.

I want you to learn stillness. True stillness, not the performance of it. I want you to stand before me and let go of every impulse to speak, to move, to fill silence with yourself. I want you to trust me enough to be empty, and to let me fill you.

This is not about the body, though the body is where we begin. It is about surrender. You have spent your whole life being asked to perform—to be clever, to be charming, to be appropriate. I am asking you to stop. To give me the woman underneath all that. The one who does not know how to be still because no one has ever asked her to be.

I am asking.

Thursday. Wear the grey dress. Do not speak when you enter. Wait for me to address you.

Yours—

M.

V.

Thursday 21st November 1887

I wore the grey dress. I did not speak. I waited.

You know what happened then. You were there. But I find I need to write it anyway, to make it real on the page, to have something I can return to in the long days before Thursday comes again.

I stood in the doorway of your workshop and I did not speak and I waited and you did not look up from your work. You knew I was there—I am certain you knew—but you did not acknowledge me. The minutes stretched. I do not know how many. I lost count. I lost everything except the waiting itself.

And then you looked up. And you said my name. Just my name, nothing else. And I understood that I had been given permission to exist again.

I did not know silence could be so full. I did not know waiting could feel like that—not empty but held. Like being cupped in someone's hands.

I am learning what you are teaching me. I think I am beginning to understand.

Yours—entirely, always—

E.

VI.

Thursday 8th December 1887

You ask what I thought when you stood before me for the first fitting. I will tell you, though I wonder if you are ready to hear it.

I thought: here is someone who does not know herself. Here is someone who has been performing for so long that she has forgotten there might be something underneath the performance. And I thought: I would like to find out what is there. I would like to strip away the layers—not of cloth, though that too—and see what remains when there is nothing left to hide behind.

This is not a kind thought. I know that. There is a selfishness in it, a hunger. I wanted to take you apart and see how you were made. I still want this. I suspect I will always want this.

But here is the thing I did not expect: I also wanted to put you back together. Differently. Better. I wanted to remake you into something that knew its own worth. That could stand still not because it was afraid to move, but because stillness was chosen. Offered. Given.

I do not know if I am capable of this. I only know that when you are with me, I want to try.

Yours—

M.

VII.

Thursday 12th January 1888

The green silk is finished. I have made the modifications we discussed—you will feel them when you wear it, though no one else will see. The boning along the left seam will press just slightly with each breath. A reminder. You asked me once how you could carry our Thursdays with you into the rest of your week. This is my answer.

You will wear the green silk to the Harcourt dinner. You will think of me when you dress, when you feel the bones against your ribs. You will sit through courses and conversation knowing what lies beneath. And when you return home—alone, as you must—you will write to me at once. You will tell me everything: how it felt to carry our secret among people who could not see it. How you sat, how you breathed, how you endured. I will not be there. But I will be holding you all the same.

Yours—

M.

VIII.

Sunday 15th January 1888

I wore it.

I sat at the Harcourt table with sixteen guests and I smiled and I made conversation about the weather and the new railway extension and Mrs. Pemberton's unfortunate choice of hat, and underneath my dress your work pressed against my ribs and I thought I might die of it.

Every breath. You were right. Every breath reminded me. Every time I shifted in my chair the weights in the hem pulled me back to you. I was surrounded by people who have known me my entire life and not one of them could see what I was wearing. What I was carrying. What I have become.

I excused myself between courses. I stood in the Harcourts' hallway with my hand pressed to my side, feeling the boning through the silk, and I had to close my eyes and breathe very slowly because I was afraid of what my face might show if anyone walked past.

No one walked past. I collected myself. I returned to the table and ate my fish course and discussed the Pemberton hat further and all the while I was yours, entirely yours, held by your work in a room full of people who could not see it.

I understand now. What you meant about carrying it with me. I understand.

Yours—entirely, always—

E.

IX.

Sunday 18th March 1888

The Harrington dinner last night. Fourteen people in the room and not one of them knew every breath I took was yours.

Mrs. Harrington commented on the dress. She said the colour suited me. She asked where I had it made. I gave her your name and your address and watched her write it down in her little book and I thought: you will go to her and she will measure you and fit you and you will never know what else those hands have done. You will never know what else that workshop has held.

I am drunk on the secret of it—sitting in those chairs and eating that food and being so entirely, invisibly yours.

Write to me. Tell me you felt it too. Tell me you were thinking of me at the moment I was thinking of you. Tell me the thread between us stretches even across town, even through walls, even when we cannot see each other.

I need to know I am not imagining this. I need to know it is real.

Yours—entirely, always—

E.

X.

Friday 4th May 1888

Thursday seems very far away.

I have been thinking about what you said—about patience, about discipline, about learning to wait without suffering. I am trying. But there is a difference, I think, between the waiting we do in your workshop and the waiting I do here, in my own rooms, with no end in sight. In your workshop the waiting has shape. It has boundaries. I know that you will end it when you are ready, and that knowledge makes it bearable. Here there is only the calendar, and the calendar does not care about me at all.

I reread your letters when it becomes too much. I have them in a box beneath my bed, tied with ribbon—I know, how ordinary, how predictable, but I could not think what else to do with them. Some nights I take them out and read them in order and it is almost like having you here. Almost like hearing your voice.

Last night I read the one about stillness. About being empty so you could fill me. And I tried to do it—to be still, here, alone, the way I am still when I am with you. I closed my eyes and I did not move and I waited for the quiet to come.

It did not come. It is not the same without you. The stillness only works when you are the one holding me in it.

I am counting the days until Thursday.

Yours—entirely, always—

E.

XI.

Sunday 12th August 1888

I am sorry I have been away. Family matters. My mother has been ill. I have not forgotten. I have not stopped thinking of you.

The weeks have been long and strange. I have sat by her bedside and held her hand and performed the role of good daughter and all the while I have thought of you. I have felt guilty for thinking of you—should I not be thinking only of her?—but the thoughts come anyway, unbidden. You are woven through me now. I cannot separate you out.

She is recovering. I will return to town next week.

Thursday. Please. I need Thursday.

Yours—always, entirely—

E.

XII.

Monday 3rd September 1888

I saw you today.

I have been thinking, all evening, of how to write about what happened. How to put into words what passed between us after so long apart. I find I cannot. The words are not large enough. The page is not wide enough to hold it.

I will say only this: I had forgotten what it was to breathe properly. I had forgotten what my body was for. You reminded me.

I am whole again. I am myself again. I am yours again.

Do not let me stay away so long. Whatever happens, whatever the world demands, do not let me stay away.

Yours—entirely, always—

E.

XIII.

Sunday 7th October 1888

You have been asking questions lately. Good questions—necessary questions. You want to understand why this works the way it works. Why you want what you want. You are searching for language, and I can feel you growing frustrated when the language does not come.

I will try to explain, though I warn you: I am better with cloth than with words.

What we do together is not about weakness. I know the world would call it that—a woman who wants to be told, who wants to give over control, who finds peace in following rather than leading.

The world has small ideas about strength. The world thinks strength means never bending.

But you know better now. You know that what you offer me is not weakness. It is trust. It is the most difficult kind of trust—the kind that requires you to set down every defence, every performance, every careful construction of self, and stand before me with nothing but your willingness to be seen.

That takes more courage than any of them will ever know.

I see you. I see what you are offering. I do not take it lightly.

Yours—

M.

XIV.

Friday 12th October 1888

You ask why I want what I want.

I do not know how to answer except to say that when I am with you, I am more myself than I have ever been anywhere else. You have shown me that what I thought was weakness—my desire to yield, to follow, to give over control—is actually a kind of strength. It takes courage to surrender. You have taught me that.

Before you, I thought there was something wrong with me. I thought the way I wanted—the way I have always wanted, even before I knew there was a name for it—was a flaw to be hidden. A shameful thing. I performed what I was supposed to want and I wondered why none of it felt real.

Now I know. Now I understand that the performance was the problem. The wanting was never wrong. It was only unspoken.

You have given me permission to want what I want. I do not know how to thank you for that except to keep giving it to you, over and over, for as long as you will have me.

Yours—always, entirely—

E.

XV.

Wednesday 19th December 1888

Christmas approaches. The house is full of preparations—my mother directing the servants, my father retreating to his study, the usual chaos of the season. I am expected to be present, to participate, to perform the role of dutiful daughter. I do my best.

But I find myself counting the hours until I can be alone. Until I can close my door and take out your letters and remember who I really am. The version of me that exists in this house—cheerful, obliging, decorating the mantels and writing cards to distant cousins —feels like a costume I am wearing. Not quite real. Not quite mine.

You are the only place I am real. You are the only place the costume comes off.

I know you cannot write as often during the season. I know you have your own obligations, your own performances. But know that I am thinking of you. In the quiet moments between festivities, in the early mornings before the house wakes, in the late nights when everyone has finally gone to bed—I am thinking of you.

January will come. Thursdays will resume. I can wait.

You have taught me how.

Yours—entirely, always—

E.

XVI.

Thursday 14th February 1889

I have always known that what we have is borrowed time. I am not of your world, and you cannot stay in mine. That does not make what we have less real. It only makes it finite.

There are conversations we have not had. Questions neither of us has been willing to ask. I see them sometimes in your eyes when you think I am not looking—the worry, the wondering, the arithmetic of how long this can last. I do not ask because I do not want to know the answer. I suspect you feel the same.

But I want you to understand something. Whatever happens—whatever the world demands of you, whatever choices you are forced to make—you will not lose what you have learned here. That belongs to you. It lives in your body now, in the stillness you have mastered, in the way you hold yourself when no one is watching. That is yours forever. No one can take it away.

I am grateful for every Thursday. I will continue to be grateful for as long as we have them.

Yours—

M.

XVII.

Tuesday 23rd April 1889

I have been trying to write this letter for three days. Every time I begin, the words come out wrong.

There are things happening that I cannot explain. Pressures, expectations, the machinery of a life I was born into and cannot escape. I feel them closing around me like the boning of a dress—but this is a dress I did not choose, made by hands that do not love me, designed to make me into someone I do not want to be.

I am frightened.

I do not know what is coming, only that it is coming. I do not know how to stop it. I do not know if stopping it is even possible.

But I know this: whatever happens, I will have had this. I will have had you. I will have had Thursdays, and the green silk, and the stillness you taught me, and the feeling of being truly, entirely known.

They cannot take that. Can they? Please tell me they cannot take that.

Yours—always, entirely—

E.

XVIII.

Monday 2nd September 1889

I understand that circumstances change. That what is possible in one season may not be possible in the next. I have asked nothing of you that you did not wish to give, and I will ask nothing now. If you need to step back from our arrangement, I will accept it. I will not make things difficult for you.

But know this: what we have built together does not disappear simply because we cease to meet. You have learned things about yourself that cannot be unlearned. You have become something that you were not before. That belongs to you now—not to me, not to our Thursdays, not to any future husband or any respectable life. To you.

Whatever happens, you will always know what it means to be truly seen.

Yours—

M.

* * *

Editor's note: No further correspondence between E. Ashworth and M. has been discovered. Eleanor Mary Ashworth married Thomas Blackwood in June 1891 and remained married until his death in 1932. She died in 1943 at the age of eighty-six. The green silk dress referenced in these letters, along with the complete correspondence, was donated to the university by her estate in 1962.

ABOUT THE AUTHOR

Rowan Bennet writes fiction about intimacy, power, and the uncomfortable spaces where people pretend they're fine.

Rowan lives in the UK.

ABOUT SECOND NEEDLE

Second Needle is an imprint dedicated to erotic fiction written with care, precision, and intent. We believe stories of desire deserve the same attention to language, character, and emotional truth as any other literary work.

Join the mailing list at: secondneedle.com

Other Books By Rowan Bennet

Chloe

Chloe owns a record shop.

She knows how to read people, how to fit herself into the spaces they leave open. It's always worked before.

When a corporate buyer circles her shop, a woman she can't quite decipher walks into her life, and the couple she loves begins planning a future she isn't sure she's part of, Chloe does what she always does—adapts. Interprets. Decides.

But some things resist being read. Some people refuse the roles they're assigned.

Chloe, Connections

Eight intimate, explicit encounters featuring Chloe, David, and Melissa.

These stories step away from the wider arc of the novel to focus on texture, chemistry, and desire.

The Colour-Coded Calendar

Six adults. Three couples. One shared calendar. No regrets.

A deputy head who needs to stop organising. An artist who sees everything. A physio who reads bodies. An architect who builds what holds. A GP who makes tea in every crisis. A teacher who guards the perimeter.

They share a school run, a WhatsApp group, and a carefully scheduled sex life that would scandalise the village if anyone looked past the colour-coding.

Nobody implodes. Nobody is punished. The calendar continues.